I0417805

J.M. WITT
MINA'S
REVENGE

Copyright 2015 © J.M. Witt
Cover Artist: Jennifer Munswami
Photographer: Darren Birks Photography
Model: Tiffany McNeil
Editor: Leticia Sidon
Publisher: J.M. Witt Books

All Rights Reserved 2015
This book may not be reproduced in any form;
in whole or in part, without written permission by
the author.
All characters and events in this book are
fictional. Any similarities to real life people and
events are purely coincidental.

Copyright © 2015 J.M. Witt
All Rights Reserved 2015
ISBN: 978-0692561515

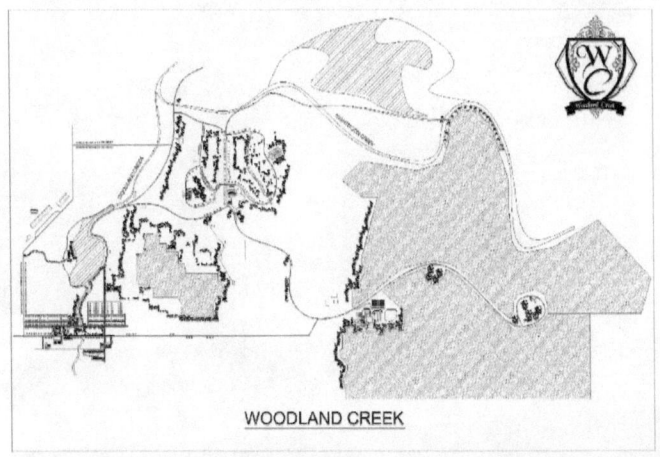

WOODLAND CREEK

For more maps and information, please visit the

Woodland Creek Website

http://woodlandcreekseries.com/

MINA

Scott had asked me to come over telling me that he had something important to discuss with me. With him you never knew if he really had something to talk about or if he was just checking up on me. Scott raised me after my mother's murder and I couldn't remember exactly when I stopped calling him 'Uncle' Scott. Maybe during high school.

He was the closest thing I had to a father, but he was either overbearing or lackadaisical. There never seemed to be anything in between. Listening to *Alive* by Sia, I took in the lyrics. It was a miracle I was still standing after all I'd been through. When the song ended I stood in my kitchen and groaned. I knew I should go see him, but I decided against it. I needed to run.

Shifting, after opening the patio door and closing it again, I took off into the woods behind my house. I ran for several hours. I was heading back to my house when I was knocked to the ground by an invisible force. Scott's face flashed in my mind and I had a horrible feeling of dread. I momentarily calculated the time to get to his place in shifter form or in my truck. The truck was the best bet. The trails between our homes was rough terrain and I'd already exhausted myself.

Quickly, I dressed and then hopped in my truck. I tried dialing his cell, but got no answer. I was growing increasingly worried. While he disliked technology, he always had his cell on him in case any of his clients needed him.

When I pulled up the drive, nothing seemed out of place. But that didn't help calm the nausea building inside me. Something was wrong. When I walked to the side door, it was already open which wasn't like him. Unlocked, yes; open, no.

"Scott? Are you here?" Walking into the kitchen, the smell of dinner lingered in the air. I was an asshole and my point was proven as I walked into the dining room to see two plates set at the table. "Nice job, Mina." After chastising myself, I continued calling his name before proceeding through the house.

His office was in the back of the house and it was in shambles. Not like it normally was; worse. Bookcases were turned over, his files scattered on the floor, and his chair tipped over. What the hell? I debated about calling the police when I thought I heard my name. Standing perfectly still, I waited to see if I heard it again.

"Mina!"

It was coming from upstairs. "Scott!"

I ran up the stairs two at a time and found him on the floor in his bathroom. He was covered in blood and I was scared stiff, literally. Images of my mother bombarded my vision. Her thin framed body laying broken on the floor, eyes open, everything red...

"Mina. Look at me." I turned my eyes toward him as he tried to calm me. "Breathe, Mina. I need you to focus."

Shaking the memory of my mother away, I cried out, "I need to call 9-1-1, you're hurt."

"There's no time for that. Come here." He pushed

himself up against the side of the tub, a bloody handprint remained when he let go.

No time? "What do you mean there's no time?"

"Mina!" He started coughing and choking on his own blood.

"Who did this? What happened?" I started panicking. I couldn't lose him the same way I had my mother. It was too much.

"Your father..." he started coughing again.

"What? My father did this?"

"Mina, stop and listen to me. Your mother wasn't the only one who died that night. I died too. You were the only thing that kept me going, the only thing I had left to live for. But, I took something from you that night."

He wheezed violently and began gagging. He was so pale. "I'm calling for help." Against his wishes, I pulled out my cell and dialed 9-1-1. After giving them the address, I set the phone down. "I'm sorry I wasn't here."

"No. I'm glad you didn't come. You could've been killed. Now listen." He pulled me closer as the tears stained my cheeks. "You need this back." He placed his hand on my chest and a surge of light blinded my vision. As I tried blinking the brightness away, he continued, "It's the only thing I have left to protect you. I'm sorry I wasn't the father you wanted."

I wasn't sure what he'd just done to me and at that moment I didn't care. He knew I was a shifter and didn't treat me any differently. As far as I knew he had no powers—at least that's what he'd always claimed— but after what he just did to me, whatever it was, I doubted him.

"You were more father than I could've asked for. I'm sorry I wasn't a better daughter." I was choking on my words as my throat constricted in response to the emotions welling inside me. He smiled and his eyes closed. "Scott! No, wake up. Please don't leave me all alone. Please."

His eyes barely fluttered open, "Trust your heart Mina. Trust R..." His head dropped.

"NO! Please. Who did this to you? Tell me." I grabbed his face and pulled him to me. "Please wake up. Trust who?" I was crying hysterically when arms pulled me from him. I fought against them, wanting to stay at his side.

The Chief of Police, TJ Rickman pulled me from the room and memories again flooded me. I was ten years old again, cops swarming my childhood home as he sat with me in his squad car. I was just a kid, but I knew him. He came into my mom's shop often and we had a bond. This time, I was in my mid-twenties, but the circumstances seemed to be the same.

"Why does this keep happening to me? Am I cursed to lose the ones I love?"

"You're not cursed, Mina. We'll find out who did this."

That made me angry and I shoved away from him. "Just like you found my mother's killer."

He sighed, "Mina, I know we've never officially closed that case, but all fingers still point to Jude Thomas."

"Yes, Jude Thomas who's never been seen or heard from since and his family lives just down the road. How do we know he's not dead too?"

One of the paramedics stepped into the hall with

us and shook his head. I knew what it meant and Chief Rickman nodded. There was no point in crying anymore. Crying got me nowhere fifteen years ago and it wouldn't get me anywhere now.

I turned to leave, but he tried to stop me. Jerking out of his reach I spit out, "I'll get my revenge. One way or another, come hell or high water, I'm going to find out who did this and they're going to pay."

"Mina..."

"If you're not going to do your fucking job then I will!"

I stormed out without a second look back.

The funeral was a few days later. The only people in attendance were fellow shifters and townspeople. The only family there was me, if you could even count me as family. I was just the kid he raised because he was infatuated with my mother at the time of her death. Standing there in the summer heat in my black dress and sunglasses on, my expression one of stone. I was numb and fine leaving it that way.

Meeting with the lawyer the next month, having

avoided it as long as I could, I found that Scott hadn't left everything to me. He'd left it to me and to a nephew of his I knew nothing about. There was only one problem. This nephew of his was contesting it since I wasn't blood or legally family and wanted it all.

I rarely heard about his family and when I had tried reaching out to them to let them know of Scott's passing, I never got my phone calls returned. Now they wanted what should've been solely mine...not that I wanted it. I had no desire or idea how to run Scott's business. Mowing lawns and plowing snow were not my idea of fun. I had my own business to run. I'd stick with the massage shop. That's what I loved.

"Mina, I can speak with them." He could sense my anger, rightfully so.

Throwing my hand in the air, I refused. "No. I have more important matters to deal with. His fucking money grubbing, greedy family can have it all. It's fine. I'll sign whatever I need to." Shoving the chair away from his desk, I stood and announced, "I have a murder to solve." The door slammed while he tried giving his warning that I should let the cops handle it. Fuck them.

They were useless. It'd been a month and there had been no new developments.

The wall went up. I didn't set foot in Scott's house again after that day. I needed to start focusing on what mattered; finding out who murdered him and why. It was time for Mina's Revenge.

ROLLO

I returned from camping in the wilderness for weeks to find out that my Uncle Scott had passed away. I hadn't seen him in years, but we kept in contact via email. When I inquired about the funeral I was informed that I'd missed that as well. I felt terrible, but there wasn't anything I could've done.

The letter I got several weeks later was what surprised me the most. Scott had apparently left everything to me. He had a business, a home on some acreage, and no one to leave it to. The only time I ever

13

saw him was when he came to visit us. I knew the reputation that Woodland Creek, Indiana had and I had to admit that I was intrigued. The town was well known in the shifter world.

It took about a month for me to close up any loose ends. My pack decided to come with me and I wasn't sure if I was happy about that or not. It came down to duty and I knew I should've felt honored that they wanted to follow me.

When I got to town and met with the lawyer, he mentioned that I sounded different on the phone and I shrugged it off. It dawned on me later that I'd never spoken with him on the phone. Deciding he must have a dozen clients he dealt with on a daily basis, I let it go.

Arriving at Scott's house, I found it in almost disrepair. There weren't any personal photographs hanging on the wall and that'd make my job a little bit harder. My cell rang and it was Victoria, my step-mother. She'd raised me since I was very young and was the only mother I remembered.

"Rollo, remember what we discussed. I know you need to get the business up and running, but she must be found. And keep her alive. I'll be there in a few months, when the eclipse happens and we'll kill her then."

"Yeah, I got it."

I disconnected the call and shoved the phone back in my pocket. It wasn't the first time I'd done Victoria's bidding or that of the pack. Though I wasn't used to keeping someone alive. Victoria prattled on about some prophecy and how this Mina girl was the key to it. She emphasized how the survival of our pack depended on it. She'd learned long ago I'd do anything to protect my pack.

Sitting down in Scott's office, I pulled out the letter that the attorney had given me. I wasn't expecting it to be from Scott personally. He mentioned his plan for me to take over the business with the girl he'd been a guardian for. This baffled me. I'd never heard anything about him caring for a girl. As the letter went on, it became obvious that he was desperate to protect her. So much so that he didn't mention her name until the end of the letter.

Mina Spitz.

Shit!

My worlds just collided. The one person Scott wanted to protect more than anything and summoned me for my help in his letter, was the one person my mother wanted wiped from this earth.

What the hell were the chances of this coincidence and how did I begin to uncover it?

MINA

Watching as the ball rolled to the destination I'd predicted, my opponent cursed.

"Shit!"

After sinking the eight ball into the corner pocket, I replaced my stick in the holder and walked over to him and held out my hand. I hadn't gotten his name and hadn't cared to. He was either new to town or just passing through, not that either mattered to me. He'd taken in my womanly shape and let his ego—and maybe the booze-- get to him. After insulting me, I'd accepted his challenge as some of the regulars looked on, giggling.

Some may have classified me as a 'shark' but that wasn't really my problem. He'd seen me as an easy win, and I proved him wrong. I could smell the stink that lingered on him. Permeating the air around me, even the aroma of peanuts and alcohol couldn't hide his stench. Of course my senses were keen and came in handy now and then. He was a shifter and I guessed a canine of some kind.

Tired of waiting, I demanded my money. "Deal's a deal. Hand it over."

He scoffed and swaggered in drunkenness as he leaned in closer. "You's a snake."

Leaning back, trying to avoid his nasty breath fanning my face, I spit out. "No, not a snake." I heard some snickers from the bar, but ignored them. "But I may go rabid on your ass if you don't hand over my money."

That seemed to get his attention. But just as quick he turned from me and stumbled toward a corner table. I stayed several steps behind as I observed those sitting there. They too were new to town or passing through. I didn't recognize any of them and I knew everyone in Woodland Creek—at least everyone who mattered.

As he took his seat, completely ignoring my

presence, my eyes immediately found a pair of green-blue eyes sitting on the other side of the table. I was momentarily drawn into them and blinked, breaking the spell. There was something about him, besides the fact that he was rugged and big. I wondered how tall he was, knowing his height had to be significant. My senses had been off lately so I couldn't get the read on him that I wanted to. His hair was long and dark and he had it pulled back loosely. His face was covered in a beard that was in desperate need of a trim. A leather coat covered his shoulders as I took in their width.

His mouth curled into a smile before he turned back to the woman hanging on his side. Rolling my eyes I turned back to my competitor. Placing my hands on the table, I leaned in and demanded my money once again.

"This is the last time I'm going to say it. You lost fair and square."

He snarled at me and the rest of the table grew silent. The ambiance changed and I stood up fully, taking a step back. My eyes met the green-blue ones once again as they shifted to gold. He was a shifter, too. Hell, probably they all were and I knew in that moment that most likely they weren't just passing through.

"Zeke, what d'ya owe the lady?"

"She hustled me, I don't owe her anything."

The same girl from before turned her attention to Zeke as she mumbled, "She ain't no lady!" She watched me, waiting for a reaction. Scouring my body, she taunted me. "In fact, I bet she works for an hourly wage on the corner."

I had a temper and before I knew it, I was nose to nose with her, leaning across the table spitting out, "You can find out how much of a lady I'm not. Just say one more word."

Green-blue eyes—my name for him—stood and everyone paid attention. He was taller than I imagined and his hair was longer, too. He walked around the table and stood in front of me. Leering down at me, his eyes flashed gold again. When I didn't flinch, his expression became curious, examining me closely. If he didn't know what I was, he was a good actor.

I was growing uncomfortable, when he suggested,

"If I were you, I'd let it go. Zeke here has a bad temper and I'd hate to see him lose that temper on a sweet thing like you."

Ugh. I was utterly disgusted. "I'm no *sweet thing*. Maybe you should warn Zeke about *my* temper."

"What's your name?" He took another step closer as I tilted my neck up to see him. If he thought he could intimidate me, he was wrong... Maybe. "Mine's Rollo." He stuck his hand between us and smiled.

Groaning, I leaned around him so my eyes could meet Zeke's. "Keep the money. Maybe use it to get groomed and bathed." Zeke lurched up, but Rollo, with a smile on his face, put his hand up and Zeke sat right back down, making it evident that Rollo was their leader.

Grinning at me he said, "You've got balls."

"If you mean bigger than his," nodding toward Zeke, I confirmed, "Bet your ass I do." It was a lost cause. Zeke could keep his forty bucks and get bent. I had more important things to deal with.

That got Rollo to smile. A chill ran up my spine and I knew I had to go. Turning, I stalked toward the door, grabbing my own leather jacket off my stool at the bar as I walked by.

I walked out of Vider's into the cold night and inhaled deeply, but another scent caught my attention. Turning, Rollo was walking out the door and headed right for me. Marching toward my store, the next one down, I picked up my pace. I didn't have time for a random hookup, not tonight.

"Hey, you didn't tell me your name."

Shouting over my shoulder, I replied, "I know I didn't."

He caught up to me and I kept on walking. "You're not cold?" Stopping, I looked at him and watched as he took in my lack of clothing appropriate for the temperatures we were experiencing. "It's cold out here."

"I could say the same to you." I picked up my pace and stopped when I stood in front of my mother's shop. Taking my keys out, I turned to face him. "Listen. I wasn't trying to hustle anyone. I won fair and square. He challenged me."

I was beginning to get nervous and wondered if

walking down the dark street at this hour with a perfect stranger was smart. I knew it wasn't. Woodland Creek had its share of mysterious disappearances and killings. I had no plan to be one of them.

He looked at the keys in my hand and up to the store. "Mora's Massage. Are you Mora?" When I didn't respond, he leaned in closer and inhaled deeply. "There's something about you, but I can't quite place my finger on it."

His fingers pulled on a strand of hair as he said it. My body began to shiver and I wasn't sure if it was from the cold or the nearness of him. A crack of lightening flashed in the sky as we both paid notice.

"ROLLO! Let's go man."

He stepped back from me and I was relieved. I could breathe again and I had a sudden urge to run. I hadn't run in shifter form in a long time, not since the night of Scott's murder, and suddenly craved it like a drug.

"See you around."

I just gawked at him as he smiled and walked away. What the hell did that mean, 'see you around'? When he was a few feet away, I unlocked the door and stepped into the safety of my mother's massage parlor.

I set things up for the next day before heading home. I didn't have any appointments scheduled but that didn't mean I wouldn't have clients. I'd been running my mom's shop—with help from Scott—for nearly eight years, though I'd only had my massage license for five. I nearly broke my back waiting tables, working odd jobs, and going to school to get it up and running again. It'd been worth it, but there were still so many unanswered questions about my mother's murder and now Scott's.

I made it home, cautious if anyone had followed me. Parking my truck in the drive, I walked into the house and then punched in the alarm code. A shower could wait. I needed to run. Stripping naked in my kitchen, I then stepped out onto the back porch. My house was secluded from prying neighbors which was the only reason I stood naked as a jay-bird out there.

I enjoyed the cold as it danced over my skin. My nipples puckered and my core ached as his eyes invaded my thoughts. Rollo. What kind of name was

Rollo? I scrubbed my face with my hands trying to shake him from my memory. He wasn't someone I should mess with. I knew it with every fiber of my being. Too bad my *being* liked fucking with and getting fucked by men like him. That was when the clouds rolled in and I could smell the rain about to come.

Closing my eyes and taking a deep breath, I shifted for the first time in months. My shifter form—black and white Siberian husky—took off like the wind into the woods. My arms and legs burned from the exertion, in a good way. I remembered running in these woods with my mother when I was young and loved and hated the memories. They were the only thing I had left of her besides the store.

I made it up a short hill and stood on all fours taking in the storm that was brewing. My senses alerted me to the presence of another being. Turning, I took a defensive stance. Staring back at me was another husky and he was red in color, something I hadn't seen since my mother. Growling at him, he stood his ground as we circled one another.

He wasn't aggressive and came closer. I was

immediately drawn to him, like an instant hunger. Curious, I tensed, but allowed him to move even closer. I didn't feel that he was a threat and let my guard down. He was a shifter, but who was he? He nuzzled up to me and before I could react I was attacked by another dog. Quickly, I got the advantage and had the bitch pinned to the ground by her neck.

Growling, I squeezed her neck a little tighter with my jaw as she whimpered. A few more huskies circled around us and I knew that I was outnumbered. All stood, teeth bared, eyes directed at me, except for one; the alpha, the one I'd been alone with for a brief moment. I watched as he walked to stand between me and the others. Releasing the neck of my would-be attacker, I backed off as she rolled to her feet and took shelter behind the other dogs.

The pack took a step toward me and he growled ferociously back at them. They backed off as he looked at me. The thunder and lightning was becoming louder and closer, matching my fear and anger as my head began to pound. Before I was attacked, had he been trying to bait me or was it purely innocent? I was dying to know who he was, but knew I had to leave.

It was as if he nodded at me, urging me to go. I wanted him to come with me, but how did I relay that without causing more problems? We were a pack breed and I had no pack, hadn't since I was young, and I wasn't looking to join one. Was I?

Running off, my head became more and more muddled making it hard to focus. The last time I'd shifted the same thing had happened and I'd woken in the middle of the night, naked, in the woods. I had to try to get home before the same thing happened. I recognized the copse of trees that outlined my property before the winds picked up and everything went black.

ROLLO

I walked away from her, leaving her in front of her store, knowing exactly who she was. What I hadn't expected was to feel about her the way I instantly did.

She was my mark—to protect and eliminate—and instead I wanted to make her mine. Fuck! Mora was long dead, along with her entire pack, supposedly. But based on the pictures I'd seen, this chick looked just like Mora. There was only one certainty; she was her daughter, Mina. This was going to complicate everything if she found out who I was, if she'd even heard of me. That had me wondering if Scott had ever mentioned me to her. According to Victoria, her mother had been a traitor, banished by both our packs and Mina was the reason for that banishment.

"Come on, Rollo. Let's run." Dixie linked her arm through mine as I brushed her off.

Dixie was determined to be mine, but I had no interest, especially when everyone had already had her. I didn't share my women. Period. Which was probably one reason I was still single. Pack life and the way I was raised battled with my own morals. I didn't want anyone's leftovers. I just wanted something that was mine and vaguely wondered how I could make Mina mine.

I hopped on my bike and as Dixie attempted to

climb on I told her to go elsewhere. We rode to my uncle's house. It'd seen better days, but it would serve its purpose and I enjoyed fixing things. I'd been in town about a week and was excited about making a new life for myself and my pack.

Walking to the backyard, I disrobed.

"Care for company?"

Looking over my shoulder at Dixie as she made no qualms of staring at my nakedness, I shook my head. "Nope. Solo run." She pouted before going back inside. She was relatively new to the pack, brought in by Zeke.

The weather was being temperamental, but I enjoyed running in the rain. Shifting, I stretched before running off into the woods. I had yet to really explore and was looking forward to it. I knew Woodland Creek was full of shifters, but had yet to have any kind of formal introductions.

A couple hours later I spotted her and began following her. I could smell her in the wind. Mina. She, too, was a husky, but black and white unlike my red. She seemed to be running alone and that made me smile. I always got grief for running solo, but there was a calmness to the solitude of running alone.

I knew the minute she sensed me. Turning, she growled to assert herself as we circled one another. Before I knew it, fucking Dixie attacked her and the whole pack was surrounding them. I was pleasantly surprised to see Mina almost immediately get the upper hand. She was scrappy and could stand her own ground.

After assuring her that my pack wouldn't harm her, she released Dixie and backed away. She seemed hesitant to leave and I wanted to go with her, but I couldn't. My pack would have serious problems with that. She ran off.

Once she was out of sight, I shifted back to human form and my pack followed suit. "I said I was running solo!" My voice boomed through the woods as the storm seemed to calm.

Dixie was massaging her neck as bruises had already started to form where Mina had clasped her. "We got worried. You've been gone for hours."

"Zeke, get your woman under control." He

nodded. "Get back to the house. I'll be there shortly."

I shifted again, taking off, and easily picked up Mina's scent. It was almost as if the storm was following her. Her trail was jagged, almost like she was drunk. When I came upon her, she was swaggering and then shifted into human form. Standing, she turned but didn't see me as I stayed in the shelter of the woods. Something was wrong with her. Her dark hair fell in wet waves over her shoulders. Her blue eyes were almost aglow, but it was like she couldn't see me, her eyes lost as rain poured down over us. It was like she had her own personal rain cloud. Was she more than just shifter? If so, what? Maybe the rumors were true that her father was a wizard.

She fell to the ground and almost as quickly, the rain ceased. I walked to her naked form lying in the grass. Nuzzling her, she was out cold. I couldn't leave her out here and shifted back into human form. Taking in my surroundings, I saw a house, the only house, about fifty feet away. There was a covered back porch and my instinct told me it was hers.

Scooping her up in my arms, I carried her to the

porch where I could smell her and laid her down on the deck. There were no blankets and the stickers on the window alerted me of the alarm she had in place. We didn't need the cops showing up now. Her lips were turning blue as she shivered. Sighing, I did the only thing I could think to do. I lay down next to her and pulled her against me.

I fought my body as it immediately reacted to the nearness of a woman. Why hadn't she reacted the way I had? I know that sounds egotistical, but I wasn't used to women not hitting on me or refusing me. Maybe she was a master of hiding her feelings. What the hell was I supposed to do now? Maybe it served me right for all the women I'd used and discarded over the years. But it'd been too long since I'd been with someone and holding her was torture. Drowsiness hit me and I couldn't help but drift off.

The slight movement of her body woke me as I leapt away from her. She was still coming to when I shifted back into husky form and walked into her yard. As she sat up, she was startled at her nakedness and probably wondering how she got to the porch. Then her eyes spotted mine and she froze.

Standing, she pleaded, "Don't go. I'll be right back."

Running into the house, I heard the high pitched warning of the alarm as she disarmed it. She reemerged on the back porch with a blanket wrapped around her shoulders.

"I know what you are and I think you know what I am. Please don't be afraid."

I took another step back toward the woods. I was pretty sure that if I shifted into human form, I wouldn't be who she expected or wanted.

"Please. Who are you?" She now stood on the bottom step and there was sadness in her voice. "I haven't seen another like us in years. Where'd you come from?"

I was enthralled by her. I wanted her. Craved to know her. Secrets, desires, needs, wants... In that moment I knew I wanted all of her. And I was going to get it. Just not right now. And there was the small problem of Victoria wanting her for her own purposes.

She stared at me as I gazed back. Sitting down,

almost in defeat, she pulled the blanket tightly around her. Covering her face with her hands, I heard her mumble something about being lonely. I was lonely, too.

Abruptly, she stood, almost as if she was embarrassed by her admission. "You know where to find me." She walked back in the house, slamming the door behind her.

Waiting, I stood on her property line as the lights downstairs turned off and the ones upstairs turned on. When all the lights were off a short time later, I left.

Over the next few days I'd go for a solo run every night in hopes that I'd run into her. But I had no such luck. I'd found no more clues at my uncle's place about Mina and wondered if what his letter had said was true. How was it that she'd lived there at some point, yet there was no evidence of it? I'd always been told that Scott had followed Mora to Woodland Creek, after her banishment, to keep an eye on her. But I was beginning to suspect there was way more to the story. And if my uncle was sent to keep an eye on her, why hadn't he returned after her death? Mina had to be the reason and if he stayed to care for her, there were a few possibilities.

The next weekend I walked into Vider's and found her hustling some college kids at the pool table. She could deny it till she was blue in the face, but she *was* a pool shark! Her eyes caught mine and she became momentarily distracted. One of the kids reminded her that it was her turn and she averted her eyes back to the table. I watched closely as she took her shot and barely made it. The boys were ogling her in the same fashion I was. Whether she knew it or not was the question.

Grinning, I flagged down the waitress and ordered drinks. "Two of whatever she's having." I pointed to Mina and the waitress nodded, though she seemed hesitant.

When she returned with the drinks, she handed one directly to Mina and whispered something in her ear before pointing in my direction. Mina lifted the bottle, smiled at me, and then took a long sip before returning to the pool game.

I sat down at the end of the bar and waited.

Chuckling at the cover song playing on the jukebox. *Maneater* by Grace Mitchell was playing overhead and I had a feeling that's exactly what she was. When the game was over, the boys groaning about how she hustled them, they handed over the money, and she made her way toward me. Standing at the end of the bar, she finished the bottle and set it down in front of me.

"Another?" She nodded. Flagging the bartender, I ordered two more.

"So. Where's your posse?"

I laughed at her question, more at referring to my pack as a posse. "Out. What about you? No posse of your own?"

Shrugging her shoulders, she answered, "I have people, you just don't know it or them."

My eyes traveled the length of the bar as eyes all the way down glanced at me. It was very clear to me in that moment that Mina was protected and valued in Woodland Creek. That intrigued me even more. My research had revealed that she'd reopened her mother's massage parlor full-time a little over five years ago. And given her young age, she'd had to bust her butt along the way. Or, she had help. I had a feeling it was probably both.

From the stories I'd heard and the digging I'd done, it was unknown who Mina's father was. I still didn't understand the rivalry my family had with hers except that it seemed someone took something that hadn't belonged to them. *That* I understood. My stepmother had raised me and had done nothing but ingrain in me the hatred for the Spitz line. As a child I didn't get it and even now I was full of mixed sentiments.

"So, Mina Spitz," that got her attention, "tell me about yourself."

She studied me before looking away and at the barmaid as they exchanged a silent conversation right in front of me. "Seems to me I don't need to. You've clearly been doing your research since I never gave you my name. All I know about *you* is that your name's Rollo. Care to enlighten me?"

The bartender set down two more bottles and we both took a drink, our eyes watching each other. My pants were growing tight with just the nearness of her and those blue eyes of hers penetrating my own.

"Rollo, Rollo Frost." That got some stares.

One of the men asked, "As in Scott Frost?"

I nodded, "He was my uncle."

"He was a good man. I'm sorry for your loss."

"Thanks."

"You planning to take over his business?"

Nodding, "That's the plan." My eyes returned to hers as she raised her eyes from my chest to my face. "Did you know him?"

"Your uncle?" She then nodded. "He was my mechanic, plumber, lawn maintenance, snow removal, and so on."

I chuckled. "Yes, he was very handy. Wouldn't know it by the condition his house is in."

"Well, he always put everyone else first," she answered. Her demeanor had changed, like she knew I was prodding and was being careful about what she said.

"True."

"Well, Rollo Frost." She downed the rest of her beer and said her goodbyes. "Time for me to go home."

Pushing herself off the bar, she headed toward the door. "Hold up." I threw down some cash, hoping it was enough and followed her. I caught up to her in the parking lot asking, "That's it?"

She laughed, "I'm sorry. Were you expecting some form of payment for the drinks?" Her question took me aback as I shook my head. "Ask Zeke to pay you. He owes me anyways."

She turned away and I grabbed her bare forearm. It was freezing out and again she was without appropriate clothing. "How are you not freezing?"

"The cold rarely bothers me. And you're not exactly wearing cold weather attire yourself."

She pointed at my long sleeve t-shirt as I smiled. "The cold rarely bothers me, as well." She tried pulling her wrist out of my grasp and instead I pulled her closer. "Mina."

Entranced once more, I took in every inch of her face. Her eyes closed as I traced my thumb over her cheek. Leaning down, my mouth was an inch from hers as her breath caught. A small groan escaped her lips as

I made her wait. That groan sealed the deal and I claimed her mouth, my hands holding her face.

Gently, I sucked on her lower lip as her hands clung to my forearms. I kept my tongue at bay until hers flicked against my upper lip. It was the only invitation I needed to invade her mouth. The kiss was hungry and brutal on both sides. Her hands moved up my arms and to my face as she fingered and pulled on my overgrown beard.

Picking her up, so I could stand to my full height, her legs wrapped around me as I pressed her against the side of a random car. I could feel every curve of her body through those black leggings and the warmth, too. Her breasts were heaving against my chest as my mouth pulled away from hers. Her eyes remained closed as she tried to steady her breath, and I tried doing the same.

Softly she whispered, "You can put me down."

"What if I don't want to put you down?" Her eyes opened and I pushed her hair from her forehead and kissed her again. She kissed me back with the same fervor from moments prior. "I don't think you want me to put you down."

Breathless, she pleaded. "Please, Rollo. I can't."

"Can't what?"

"Can't do this…"

Her hands and mouth contradicted her plea. Pulling the shirt from the waist of my jeans, her hands moved over my abdomen and through my chest hair. She kissed me with an eagerness that demanded my attention. Maybe she did recognize that there was something between us, but why were her words denying it?

"Mina…" Fuck, I wanted her. She pressed her hips against me and I could feel her warmth through the denim of my jeans. "Christ. Let's go somewhere."

"I, what? No." She didn't stop kissing me and I was becoming amused and annoyed with her. Did she want me to take her in the parking lot? Because I would. Her words were refuting me while her actions were egging me on.

Pulling us apart, I set her back on the ground. Holding her shoulders between my hands I questioned her. "Mina, make up your mind. What do you want?"

Sighing, she shook her head. Glancing in my eyes she crushed me with her words. "Not this."

"What the hell does that mean?" Immediately I was on the defense.

"No, that's not what I meant. Shit." She ran her hands through her hair and took a deep breath. "You're the right kind of wrong and I can't do this with you. Not like this. I'm done with random hookups and I don't have time for a relationship."

Tilting my head at her I tried figuring her out. It seemed my powers of persuasion had no effect on her. Not that I wanted to persuade her to sleep with me, but I did want to persuade her to tell me the truth. So she was used to random hookups, but was done with them? She wanted to hookup, but not this quick, not in a parking lot? I wasn't into playing games and I was beginning to think that she was.

"Honey, you're going to have to spell it out for me. I want you, you want me." Leaning in I whispered, "I can smell it on you."

She gaped at me and spit out, "Don't talk to me like I'm a bitch in heat!"

Grinning, I couldn't resist retorting, knowing what I knew. "Aren't you?"

Her face immediately turned red as thunder boomed from above. Her hand lifted and I stopped her just before she made contact with my face. "Fuck you. This is exactly why this can't and WON'T happen."

She shoved me away from her and hurried toward her truck. "Mina, wait. I'm sorry. This can happen, it WILL happen."

Jumping in her truck she yelled, "Prove it!" She slammed the door and then peeled out of the parking lot, leaving me staggering back to avoid getting side-swiped by her truck.

"Shit!" Prove what? That I was sorry or that this would happen?

MINA

What the hell was wrong with me? 'Prove it!' Why had I said that and what did I want him to prove? I didn't have time for this, for him, especially finding out that he was Scott's nephew. FUCK! I needed to get back to trying to find out who killed Scott and who it was he was trying to tell me to trust. Then there was the issue of who my father was and who murdered my mother. It'd been almost fifteen years, but something else was going on with me. I was having blackouts, mostly after shifting and suspected it had something to do with my father. I didn't have time for Rollo and the devastation he would cause my heart.

Part of me was furious with my mother thinking she may have known something about my father and never told me. I was only ten when she was killed. And

I'd lied to Rollo about his uncle just being my mechanic. Did Rollo know Scott was my legal guardian? Ugh. I had been a rotten teenager and though I made it incredibly difficult on him, he'd offered to adopt me on more than one occasion, but I'd refused.

Scott knew what I was and never judged me for it. The only thing he'd ever mentioned was that he was from a shifter family, but hadn't inherited the gene. Now that I thought about it, he'd never mentioned family of his and I didn't recall him ever leaving to visit relatives. If Rollo was here to take over his business how come I knew nothing about it, about him?

Something was off. Maybe Rollo wasn't really his family. Scott and I hadn't talked very much prior to his death and I regretted that. His attorney had told me about Scott's nephew and yes, I'd just handed everything over willingly. I didn't think anything of it except that if I'd let Scott adopt me, I'd have been the relative in charge of all of it. But, I was just some brat he took care of who never appreciated him the way I should've.

When I pulled into the cemetery, I got out of my

truck and headed to where he was buried. A headstone had been ordered, but it wouldn't be finished for months. I sat down and let my emotions take over. Not something I did often. He was the closest thing I had to a father and I'd treated him like crap.

A storm moved in and I was beginning to feel like I had an eternal rain cloud following me. A surge ran through me as I closed my eyes. Fighting it off never did any good, instead it almost made it worse. Another blackout was coming, the migraine that preceded them was making its way up my spine. The cracking of a branch alerted me that I wasn't alone. I inhaled deeply, but my sense of smell was off. In fact, I couldn't remember what Rollo smelled like and I had just been with him. Something was terribly wrong with me.

Turning my head, I saw him. The red husky had returned. I knew I was safe with him—though his pack was another question—but I wanted to know who he was. Returning my face to Scott's grave, the husky came to sit next to me as I wiped the lingering tears from my face. I was trying to catch my breath when he placed his head on my lap and I lost it all over again.

"I miss him so much. I was horrible to him and all he did was love me like a father should love his child. Yet, I denied him that right." Inhaling and exhaling shakily, "But I wasn't his child. My mother is gone, my father a mystery. Something's happening to me and I don't know how to stop it, or even what it is."

Another crack of thunder boomed from above as we both looked up. I outstretched my arms as the rain began to fall, silently wishing lightning would strike me down. Then there wouldn't be any more worries about who killed Scott, my mother, or who my father was.

I heard him whine and looked to him. He stood and started running in small circles, wanting me to play with him. I just shook my head.

"I can't. I can already feel it coming. If I shift I'll black out." He barked toward my truck and I looked between the two. "This is crazy. I'm talking to a dog like you can understand me." He barked and growled at me knowing I was taunting him, and then sat down on his hind legs, glaring at me. "Ok. I don't know why you won't just show me who you are." Nothing. "Do I know you?" Nothing. Sighing, "Ok. I'm going home. If you are what I think you are, you'll meet me there."

I stood up as he nuzzled up against my side. He was big, his shoulders reaching my waist. Stroking his head and scratching behind his ears, he leaned into me. After a moment, I headed toward my truck and climbed in. He barked at me and I reiterated my words.

"You know where to find me." Then I drove off. His image stared at me in the rearview mirror and part of me wanted him to shift, but instead he ran off into the woods. "I'm truly losing it. Now I've resorted to talking to stray dogs that I think are shifters."

I got home and headed to the kitchen. Starving, I pulled some lunchmeat out of the fridge and made a sandwich. I was startled when I heard barking on my back porch. Turning the light on, I peered out the sliding door and there he was, my stray red husky. I opened the door and he cautiously stuck his nose in the door.

"You better be housetrained." He snarled and I giggled. "Just saying. Don't shit on my floor or try marking your territory." He buried his head in my crotch as I pushed him away. "Hey! Knock it off." He sat down and stared at the last of my sandwich. "Begging huh? You hungry?" I threw the remainder of my sandwich in the air and he caught it, inhaling it down.

When he was done licking his lips he started pacing. I raised my brows and sat down at my small dining table. Gently, he put my foot in his mouth and pulled on it. He wanted to go run and I shook my head. He barked so loudly, I jumped.

"I told you, if I shift I'm going to black out. You prepared to carry me back here?" He barked again as I scratched my head. "Alright. I'll take that as a yes. Turn around." He growled as I raised my brows. "I'm not stripping in front of you."

He stepped back through to the porch, keeping his back to me. I stripped my clothes and walked through the door, closing it behind me. Shifting, I then rammed my head into his side, throwing him off balance, and took off in front of him. We ran for a few hours and I didn't black out. Instead, I passed out from exhaustion.

This went on for a couple of weeks. Each time I woke with him next to me. Sometimes I was in shifter form and others in human form, but he always remained in shifter form. I didn't see much of Rollo, but when I did he kept his distance, and that was fine with me.

I came home from work every night, avoiding Vider's, hoping to find Red—that's what I named him—waiting, and most nights he was there. I sat on the back porch as the first snow began to fall with his head on my lap. It was early for snow and that's when it dawned on me it was Halloween. I groaned and he lifted his head to look at me.

"Don't look at me that way. You're giving me a complex. You need to show me who you are or I stop this." He whined in response. "This is crazy. You know more about me than anyone and I don't even know who you are."

He jumped up and pushed me down, pinning me and licking my face.

"Hey, stop it! I'm not a fan of doggy kisses, not when I'm in human form." My cell rang and I pushed him off of me as I got up to answer it.

It was Debi. She had the night off and wanted me

to meet her at Vider's for their annual Halloween gathering. It was funny how even on her night off she spent it in the bar. I needed the girl time. Debi was a shifter, too. Maybe she was just who I needed to talk to.

"Ok. Give me a few. I'll meet you there." I slid the phone in my pocket as Red whined. "Not tonight. I'm going out." Walking through the sliding door I went to close it as he tried coming inside. "Nope. Until you're ready to reveal yourself, this stops."

I shut the door as he stared back at me. Hesitantly, I turned the light off and closed the curtains. Why did I feel guilty? This was ridiculous. Opening the curtains again, he was gone. I changed my clothes, freshened up, and headed back into town. I'd grabbed my devil horns and that would have to suffice for my costume.

I found Debi in the corner playing pool and made my way over. Dressed as a cheetah, also her shifter form, I laughed at the irony. She was flirting with some college boys as I tried ignoring it. We weren't that much older than them, but it was just not my M.O. Debi could have her fun, but I wasn't interested.

An hour later, the door to the bar opened and there he was. My panties immediately soaked at the memory of our last encounter. His eyes met mine as he smiled. There was no denying I wanted him. But the minute Dixie sidled up next to him, I wanted to vomit, or punch her in the crotch. If they weren't a couple he was doing everything to make me think otherwise. I couldn't be with someone who shared his women and wasn't loyal. I knew she was with Zeke, too. I wanted to belong to one man, no one else. Someone who was willing to make me his and announce it to the world.

Debi elbowed me and whispered, "If you don't stake claim on him, I will."

"Don't you dare!"

She pointed her finger in my face, "I knew it! You have a thing for him."

Groaning, "Ugh. It's purely carnal and not going to happen. I mean, look at him. Women are falling all over themselves." He was surrounded by a flock of women and I found it infuriating and repulsive. I envisioned myself walking over and staking my claim, but it was preposterous.

"Carnal is what we do, Mina. Is he what you want?"

Her question surprised me. Shaking my head, "I don't know. Everything is all screwed up in my head."

She nodded. I'd told her about Red, Rollo being Scott's nephew, the headaches, and the blackouts. She had told me if Red wasn't willing to reveal himself to me that he wasn't worth my time. She thought Rollo was time worthy. I thought differently.

"Well, you're hot and by the way he's looking at you, he wants you, too, Mina."

I just shook my head. "He's trouble with a capital T."

"That's what makes it so much fun." She giggled and ordered us some shots then headed to the jukebox. When she came back I asked her what song she picked and she just said, "You'll know when you hear it."

I didn't get another chance to talk to Debi like I wanted and maybe it was for the best. Rollo and I kept stealing glances at one another and a few minutes later *Monster* by Lady Gaga came on. I knew it was the song Debi had picked. She had a twisted sense of humor. I downed one shot after another, staring at Rollo, our eyes never parting as the song played.

We were playing a game of chicken, waiting for the other to make the first move, and both too stubborn to do it. Instead we'd end up crashing into each other at some point and the aftermath was sure to be fatal.

I drank too much and let a couple of frat boys get a little too grabby with me and Rollo tried stepping between us.

Pushing him away, I declared, "I got this." He ran his hand through his hair, mumbling something I missed before walking away.

Debi had disappeared, probably out back or headed to the dorms or her place. I knew I should go. I knew it wasn't a good idea for me to drive, so I'd just crash at my shop. Thank God for the couch in the back office.

Stumbling out the door, I made my way through the parking lot.

"Mina!"

Fuck. "Go away, Rollo." A sudden cold wind blasted us as he caught up to me.

"You're not driving."

Dangling the keys in front of him, I stated the obvious. "Duh. I'm going to my shop. I'm fine. Go. Away!"

"You told me to 'Prove it'. What did you mean?"

My head hurt at the thought of it all and it was instantly sobering. Looking up to him, I lost focus and just stared at him. "I, oh, never mind." I turned back toward the shop when his hand captured my arm.

I didn't fight him as he pulled me close. "No. I need to know."

His warmth was soothing as the temperatures dropped around us. "That was weeks ago, Rollo. You have your pick of women. Go bother one of them."

"I don't want one of them. I want you."

Christ on a cracker, I'd fall over if he let his hold on me go. "You're just saying that. I know your kind all too well. It's all about the challenge, the victory, and then you drop me like a sack of potatoes." He lifted his chin as his eyes looked down upon me, studying me. "Stop looking at me that way." I backed up against the brick wall and knew I was trapped.

"What way?"

"Like you're going to devour me."

"That's exactly what I plan to do, sweetheart." He pressed his body against mine. "This isn't a one-time deal for me." He nuzzled my neck as a chill ran up my spine.

"What if I said it was for me?"

Grinning, "One time will never be enough and you know it."

He threw me over his shoulder and asked for the keys to my shop. I handed them over and he opened the door. All the fight in me was gone. Just one time. I'd be his for one night. It would have to be enough to last a lifetime because a lifetime was too long for anything to last. Lord help me.

ROLLO

Over the past few weeks I found out things I never

knew about both our families. I got confirmation that my uncle Scott had actually raised Mina after her mother's death. How was it that I'd never known that before? I'd heard the rumors that he was in love with Mora and now I believed it. I began to wonder if there was a chance he was Mina's father and the possibility was definitely there, but it didn't explain the powers that resided in her. There was so much mystery surrounding all of it and I had to know why.

Scott was my father's brother, though they weren't blood. Scott had been adopted in by my grandparents and did not have the shifter gene. So even if he was Mina's father, there was no blood connection between Mina and me. Thank God. But it sure would've made for interesting conversation. I was thinking about things like I had already planned our future. Maybe part of me had.

I'd spoken with Victoria and asked questions without trying to make her suspicious. Victoria was still adamant of her hate of the Spitz line and I just didn't understand why and began questioning everything I'd ever been told.

I had to be careful because she was also Zeke's mother. A child my father welcomed to the family and raised as his own. Zeke was more than my best friend, we were raised as brothers. Now I was suspicious of everyone and everything, including Zeke. Except Mina. She was something and someone I had complete faith in. But why did my stepmother want her dead? I never questioned doing the bidding of my family, until now. Scott was adamant in his letter that I should protect Mina, but it was killing me that he hadn't elaborated.

I'd spent almost every evening with Mina in my shifter form. Every time she asked me to show her who I was, it got harder and harder to resist. Tonight had been no exception, but I knew she just wasn't ready for it, couldn't handle it. And I wanted her to want my human form more. I was playing a dangerous game and I knew it.

Now, walking into her massage shop with her over my shoulder, all my plans to make her wait, to woo her properly, had been pushed aside. Closing the door behind me and locking it back up, I let her slide down my front. She stepped back from me, her nerves taking over as I took in my surroundings.

She had a pretty good setup. Oils, lotions, and other items lined the wall behind the counter. There was a sign with the types of massage listed along with their price.

"So, if I wanted a massage would you be my therapist?"

She gaped at me before shutting her mouth. "Yes, I'm the only therapist."

Removing my leather coat and dropping it on the counter, I asked, "Have any openings? I'm awfully sore." She just stared at me dumbfounded as I smiled. "I can pay."

"I, you want a massage. Now?"

"Why not? No better time." I winked at her.

Shrugging her shoulders, she surprised me with her reply. "Follow me." We walked into the room on the left as she turned the light on. "It's going to take a minute to warm up." She turned on the heating pad on the table and laid down some blankets over it.

"I'm pretty warm. I'll be fine."

Smiling, "I'm sure you are." I started getting

undressed as she turned toward the door. "Get under the covers, I'll be back in a minute."

I stripped down to my birthday suit and got on my back under the sheet. The lighting was soft and music played gently. I'd asked around town where the best place was to get a massage and everyone mentioned Mora's Massage, claiming Mina was amazing. It was time to find out. Some even joked that she had magical power. Little did they know.

The door opened as she asked, "Are you ready?"

"I should ask you the same question."

I saw her shake her head as she stood next to me. "Do you have any allergies or scents you dislike?" I shook my head no. "Any pain or injuries I should know about?"

"An old shoulder injury, but it's hopeless. I've had three surgeries. Nothing helps."

"Ok." She walked over to a shelf with dozens of little brown vials with colored labels on them and grabbed a few. "Do you prefer oil or lotion?"

"Uh, you're the expert."

"Oil it is. It goes further and lasts longer." I arched

my brows at her and she just scoffed. "Close your eyes and relax." Closing one eye, I watched as she mixed some oils together and then put some in her hands. She caught me watching her and chastised me. "Rollo! This isn't going to work if you don't relax."

"Yes ma'am."

Closing my eyes, I took a deep breath as she took my hand in hers and began running her hands up and down the length of my arm. When she was done with that arm she moved to the other and started over. She'd only just begun and I was becoming putty on the table. Moving to the head of the table, she began working over my neck and shoulders after putting more oil in her hands. Her oil-slick fingers moved over my pecs and back into my long hair.

Massaging my temple, I groaned and I sensed her smile as she asked, "When's the last time you had a professional massage?"

"Would you believe me if I said never?"

"Yup. Most people don't indulge themselves. Now you know what you're missing."

"Hmmm."

After she was done massaging my head she moved down to my feet. I was slightly jumpy as she discovered how ticklish my feet were. I told her she might need to skip over my feet when she refused.

"Deep breaths, Rollo. Relax."

She worked her way up each thigh as I tried controlling my body's response to her. If she noticed, she didn't say anything. My eyes fluttered open when I felt her standing above me and the sheet lifted slightly.

Meeting her eyes, she said, "You can roll over now, though it might be a little uncomfortable." Her head motioned toward my cock that was standing at full attention under the sheet.

"Christ. Sorry."

"No you're not. But it's ok. It's pretty common."

Her eyes remained on mine as I rolled over, until I buried my face in the cutout. She pulled my hair to one side as my eyes stared at her bare feet. I wasn't aware she'd removed her boots, but didn't think about it. I spotted the script on the inside of her foot that ran along the top of her arch and was curious to what it said. It was the first time I recalled seeing it.

I winced as she massaged my left shoulder. "I take it this is the shoulder?" I moaned in agreement as she grabbed some more oil. "I can help, but it's going to hurt."

"I already told you, nobody can help it."

"Ye of little faith." She began applying pressure and asked, "Do you trust me?"

"I barely know you."

"Rollo."

"Whatever you're going to do, just do it." She stepped away for a moment and pressed something heavy and hot onto my shoulder. Before I knew it, I was cursing. "FUCK."

"Lie still. I'm almost done." I did as she told me as the pain slowly subsided. "There. Let it rest for a minute while I check your other shoulder."

I don't know what the fuck she did, but it was helping. Pain that had nagged me for years was melting away as she worked on my other shoulder. I'd heard the rumors of her mother's healing powers. Apparently Mina had inherited those, too.

"That's not a common injury, Rollo. What'd you

do?" I shrugged my shoulders, refusing to answer. "When are you going to tell me what you are?"

So she suspected or was she baiting me. "You can't handle what I am."

"What makes you so sure?"

Time to turn the tables on her. "What are you, Mina?"

"I don't know what you're talking about."

"Exactly. You're not ready for me to reveal all of myself to you either."

"Maybe you're right." She was working on my lower back and asked, "Do you mind if I climb up?"

"Can I roll over first?"

Laughing, "No. I need to finish your back, and, well, it's easier if I'm on top of you."

"Yes, it is easier with you on top."

Humor laced her voice as she told me to knock it off. She climbed up and began kneading my back as she straddled my upper thighs.

"Christ woman."

"Shh. Relax."

I let her work on me for a few minutes. When I

couldn't stand it anymore I rolled over, grabbing her hips so that she didn't fall off the table. She drew her hands to her chest as I sat up, only the sheet separating us. I could smell her arousal and it was making me crazy with the need to get her off. My own hunger could wait. Leaning up, I buried my face in her neck, and her chest heaved as I sucked and nipped on her flesh.

"Mina. Let me prove that this is more than a hookup." She whimpered in my mouth when I kissed her. Pulling my mouth away, I asked, "Can I return the favor?"

She seemed confused and wiggled closer to me. "What favor?"

I pushed her off me and put her feet on the floor before standing. The sheet dropping to the floor, her eyes dropped to my erection as she gulped. "Eyes up here, Mina." Blushing, her eyes slowly returned to mine. "Get undressed. I'm going to guess you haven't had a massage in a long time and I'd like to remedy that."

She rarely came off as shy and reserved, but she

seemed so at that moment. "This wasn't what I had in mind when we came in here." And there she was. My blunt and up front girl, not the shy one.

Laughing, "Me either. We've got all the time in the world."

"No. We have tonight. One night, Rollo. That was my agreement."

Stepping closer to her, I cupped her chin, "I plan to convince you otherwise."

I had a feeling there was a vixen in her dying to get out. She just needed the right man to do it and I would happily oblige. She may have tried to occasionally play coy with me, but she was anything but. Pulling her closer, I dropped my mouth to hers and consumed her. I didn't stop until her whimpers resounded through my own mouth.

"If you only want one night with me, Mina, you better make it count. Don't hold back; you'll only regret it if you do." She groaned as her hands dug into my back, pulling me closer. Biting my lip, she sucked it into her mouth until it throbbed to the same rhythm as my cock. "There she is."

MINA

Lord almighty he was beautiful. I'd never wanted to get my hands on someone more. I thoroughly enjoyed massaging every inch of him until he threw me off of him. I wanted to lose all control, throw my inhibitions to the wind, and get lost in him. And I had a feeling he knew.

"There she is."

His hands pushed under my t-shirt and scorched my skin. Hot, callused hands ran over my delicate flesh as I dueled with his tongue. We parted long enough for my shirt to get yanked over my head and dropped to the floor.

"Rollo..."

He pushed me to arm's length and said, "Get undressed and under the covers. I'll be back." I watched as he grabbed the sheet, his clothes, and left the room.

"Fuck. Get it together, Mina. This isn't your first rodeo."

Though I knew he'd be more than an eight second ride and I wasn't sure I would be able to stay on. Christ, he was hung. I shook the thought away—for a moment—and got undressed. My nipples were hard and aching and my panties clung to me as I pulled them from my damp skin. He was right, anyone who walked into the room would smell my arousal. I sat on the table and realized he'd taken the sheet with him.

Getting up, I went to grab another from the cabinet when the door swung open. I stood there naked as he took in my body. He was wearing underwear and I felt entirely exposed.

"Sorry, I realized you might need this." He held the sheet up between us and I snatched it from him and covered myself with it. I sat on the table and watched him. He closed the door and then examined the oils. "Do you have a preference?"

"Oil." I pointed to a bottle and he picked it up.

"Aren't you supposed to be lying down?" Exhaling loudly, I did just that, holding the sheet to my neck. Mocking me, he said, "Relax, Mina. I'm not going to do anything you don't beg me to do. Outside the massage that is."

Snickering, "Is that so?"

"Yup. Now shut up and relax."

I smiled as he attempted to mimic my movements. He began with my hands and arms, working his way up to my neck. Rubbing my neck and shoulders, he hesitated just above my breasts. 'Better make it count'. I pushed the sheet to my waist, exposing my breasts to him. His eyes met mine and I nodded before closing them again.

End Of All Days by Thirty Seconds To Mars began playing from my playlist. Applying more oil to his hands, he slowly worked down and over my breasts. I couldn't contain the moan that escaped from my mouth. It'd been too long since I'd been touched like this, if ever. I felt the heat of his massive body as he leaned over me. Opening my eyes, I found his chest hovering over me.

His hands ran over my hips as I nearly convulsed off the table from him hitting a sensitive spot. He moved back up and when his mouth hovered over mine, I pulled him down, needing his mouth on mine. Digging my nails in his hair as his hands caressed my breasts, he resisted, not letting his lips touch mine.

Gasping, pleading, "Rollo, kiss me."

"Ask nicely."

"Rollo, please kiss me. Now."

Grinning, he lowered his mouth to mine, our lips misaligned as he let me lead the kiss. His fingers tweaked my nipples as I pressed my breasts up into his rough hands. One hand moved down and over the sheet between my legs. I became paralyzed as his eyes locked with mine. Pressing his hand over my lips, I clamped my thighs around his hand and shifted my hips. My eyes rolled back and closed at the wonderful sensations shooting through me.

"Roll over." I tried protesting, but he silenced me with his kiss. "Now, roll over."

I did his bidding and he did the same. Straddling my thighs as he began working over my shoulders and

71

back. I was hanging in limbo between pure ecstasy and wanting to sleep. His fingers moved over a ticklish spot on my hips and he caught it.

Moving back over the spot, he questioned, "Was it here, or here?"

Squirming under his touch, he stopped and resumed massaging my lower back. I felt his lips place kisses on my back as his tongue moved along my skin. One hand moved under the sheet, between our bodies as he ran it over the crease of my ass. I tried to remain still, but he was making it increasingly difficult.

Lifting my head I turned it back and found his eyes. Gripping my hair, he yanked it back and growled at me. "Don't look at me that way, Mina."

I pulled back against his grip, enjoying the feel of his hand in my hair. "What way?"

"Like you want me to devour you."

Smiling wickedly, "That's exactly what I want, Rollo."

Tugging on my hair once more, I moaned with the pleasure of it as he attacked my mouth. "I think I was right."

"About?"

"I'll tell you later." He kissed me again. His hand moved underneath me to my front and I lifted slightly to grant him access. His hand dipped between my legs and found my wet pussy. Bringing his fingers back up to his lips, he licked his fingers and then kissed me. "Devour." He enunciated every letter in my ear before climbing off the table.

The sheet was ripped off my legs as his hands encircled each calf and began kneading them. He didn't waste any time as he moved up my thighs. The thought of him staring at my pussy turned me on even more. His hands grabbed my ass cheeks and pulled them apart as he exposed every part of myself to his prying eyes.

Gripping my ankles, he pulled me to the edge and then ordered me to get on my knees. I had a feeling I knew what was coming and I was dying from anticipation. His teeth dug into my ass as I dropped my chin to my chest. I felt his hot breath on my skin and began trembling.

"Beg me, Mina."

Taken aback for a split second, I decided that I

J.M. Witt

didn't care how desperate I sounded. I wanted him more than anything I'd ever wanted before. "Eat me, Rollo. Devour me. Please."

His scorching hot mouth dove onto my pussy with such force that I had to grip the table to hold on. It was almost too much all at once. My mind didn't have time to catch up to the sensations he had ripping through my body.

"Rollo, slow down. Please." His tongue slowed and licked in long luxurious strokes from my clit to my ass. "Oh, God." He took his time as my whole body continued to tremble. I needed this release, wanted it, craved it, but it wouldn't come.

"What is it, Mina? What's wrong?"

"I need...more. More of *you*."

He seemed to know what it was I needed before I could verbalize it. Sliding a finger inside, he motioned it toward my g-spot as I cooed. I rocked back and forth against his hand before he removed it. Pulling on my hair again, he moved to stand next to me before he kissed me. Sucking viciously on my lips, he slapped my ass with his free hand.

I'd never felt so dirty—in a sexy way—ever in my life. I wanted to lose all abandon with him, maybe I already had. My hips began to swivel, desperate for him to touch me again. I was shocked motionless when he grabbed me like a six pack. Gasping as his fingers began to move in and out of me, my back slackened as I let the sensations move through me again.

"Tell me what you want, Mina." He demanded it of me, what I wanted, like he was going to give it to me, but I knew better. He was enjoying his game—I was too—and he was only going to give me what he wanted to. But there was no point in not asking for it.

"I want to come."

"How, where?"

Two fingers pumped in and out of me slowly as I moaned. "On your cock, on your face... I just want to come. Please make me come, Rollo." Oh, my God. Did I just say that out loud?

"You can't have my cock. Not tonight." So that was his plan to get me to beg for another night? He was going to withhold his enormous dick. I whimpered. Reminding me, he whispered in my ear, "I told you one

75

night would never be enough."

Before I knew what was happening, he'd lain down under me and gripped my hips as I grasped his shoulders. I'd never had a man this way—sitting on his face—before and wasn't sure where to begin.

"What are you waiting for? My face is all yours. Ride it, fuck it, grind it…" He waggled his tongue at me as my lips curled up.

He was so salacious and I loved it. Slowly, I moved my mound closer. Sitting on his chest, his head lifted to lick me fully. "Oh, shit."

His tongue slid inside me as I tried to get closer to him, but also worried about smothering him. He moaned his appreciation so I pressed into him further. Hands caressed my legs, hips, and ass as I became desperate for more of him. Leaning up, I began riding his face as I gripped his hair. My other hand reached behind me in search of his cock. Finding the head poking through the waistband of his boxer briefs, I stroked him.

Smiling up at me he pulled back long enough to encourage me on, "Yes, Mina, just like that." Was he referring to my hand stroking him or me fucking his face?

I didn't care. "Shut up and lick me, Rollo."

"Shut up and fuck me, Mina."

He pulled me down fully on his face. His tongue thrusting in and out of me while his nose pressed into my clit. He was throbbing in my hand and I wanted to get him off, maybe as bad as he wanted to get me off. Moving my hips, I slid up and down his tongue letting it glide over every part of me. His beard did wonders to my throbbing clit as I rubbed it against his chin.

"I'm close. Rollo." I became frenzied, desperate to not lose what was about to happen. My fist tightening in his hair, I let go wholly. I fucked his face like there was no tomorrow. "Ahh. Now…" He licked and sucked me until the only part of me that was left moving was my hand on his shaft.

"Mina. Fuck." He groaned out as his seed shot out against my back and into my hand.

He'd been closer than I thought he was. His eyes flashed gold and then back to his green-blue as he panted out his appreciation. I was completely lost,

J.M. Witt

entirely sated. That had never happened, yet I wanted more.

I didn't want to think about what time it was. The night would be over soon and I was already craving more of him. He cleaned off my back, tucked himself back in his underwear and carried me to the couch in the back office. Laying me down, he covered me with a blanket and turned toward the door.

"Don't go." Ugh, I didn't mean to sound so needy.

"You just wanted one night, Mina." He motioned toward the window. "Sun's coming up. Time for me to go." He smiled back at me and challenged, "Unless you have something to say?"

Fuck him if he thought I was going to admit that I needed more than one night. He could fucking beg *me* for another night. "Clearly I don't need your dick to get off!"

"No, you don't. Just me. My face, my tongue, my hands, my fingers. They can all get you off. So just imagine what my dick could do to you, sweet Mina."

He was infuriating. "You won't get a chance to find out! You know where the door is."

Sighing, "You're a stubborn ass."

"Ok. Admit that you want another night, too." We were in a stand-off.

"That wasn't part of the bargain, Mina. I already told you this wasn't a one night deal for me."

"Please. Dixie won't let this happen again once she finds out."

He laughed. "If you think that hussy has any say over what and who I'm with, you're wrong. I've never done to her what I just did to you, what you begged me to do. Not even close. I don't share what's mine, make no mistake, and she was *never* mine."

I flinched at the harshness in his voice. Was he trying to say that I was his? I didn't know what to say or do. Standing, I followed him out of the room. He was throwing his clothes back on as I watched him dress. I blocked the door and he picked me up and moved me like a ragdoll. I didn't want him to go, but I couldn't get myself to say the words.

"I'm not into playing games, Mina. When you're ready to admit what's here, I hope for your sake I'm still around."

The front door slammed behind him. Crushed, I locked the door and went back to the office and curled up on the couch. What happened? What did I just do? I wasn't even sure what went wrong. His ego, mine, I wasn't sure. There was one thing I had most certainly been wrong about. One night with him would never be enough to satiate me. It didn't even begin to scratch the surface for the hunger he'd now instilled in me.

The next evening I walked out on to my back porch and found a note on the patio for me. A brick held it down and my name was written on top. I looked around my back yard and didn't see anyone and nothing seemed out of place. Picking up the letter, I took a shaky breath and opened it up.

Dearest Mina,

Please forgive me for being hesitant in revealing myself to you. I am what you believe me to be. Know that I have treasured our time together and the secrets you've revealed to me will stay just that; secrets.

Writing this letter has been one of the hardest things I've ever done. I've never felt for anyone what I feel for you. I can't explain it, but it's more than a feeling. It's an instinct, a belief, an intuition that you're meant to be mine.

I hope that I haven't waited too long and that you'll give me another chance. And please, when I do reveal myself to you, know that I had my reasons for waiting.

Yours truly,
Red

I collapsed in the patio chair knowing what I'd done. In going to the bar that night with Debi, I'd quite possibly ruined whatever it was I was building with Red. By indulging with Rollo, I'd opened Pandora's Box. Emotions now flooded me for two men, one who knew me carnally and the other who knew me emotionally. How could I ever choose between them?

ROLLO

What had just happened? I stood outside her

shop, baffled. I heard the click of the lock and knew she wouldn't let me back in. Not tonight. I tuned my ears to her movement as she walked to the back office. Her gentle sobs began to fill my ears and I couldn't stand to listen to them. Hopping in my truck, I drove home as the sun rose. I slept most of the day away. After waking, I decided to head to her place to see if the letter I'd left for her was still sitting on the patio table where I'd placed it.

I was having second thoughts about writing it and hoped she hadn't found it yet. I wasn't some teenage boy writing a love letter. What the hell had I been thinking? I had written it last night before I headed to the bar to check in on her. I meant every word of that letter and that's what scared me the most. *Nightcall* by Kavinsky was playing again and I made a mental note to update my playlist.

When I drove by her place, her truck was out front. Parking down the block, I headed into the woods and circled back behind her property. Standing at the tree-line on her property, I'd arrived too late. She was reading the letter, her hand clutching the shirt she wore just above her heart. I nearly blew my cover when she dropped into the chair and began sobbing.

I was pretty sure I knew what was running through her head, which was part of why I wanted to get the letter back before she read it. She felt loyalty to us both, my red husky shifter form and me, as Rollo. I shouldn't have taken her back to the massage shop. In doing so I'd made her feel cheap and used, or so I assumed. But another part of me told me that her guilt was a good sign. She cared about me, both parts of me.

I kept my distance the next couple days. Meeting with a local PI, we continued looking more into her background. We pulled birth certificates, death certificates, and found nothing. No father was listed. We scoured the newspapers during the timeframe of her mother's death. Jude Thomas had been a suspect, but he hadn't been seen since the night Mora's body was discovered. And from the details, there was a second body at the scene, but not enough to I.D. it. Speculation said that it was Jude, but DNA tests didn't match. Whoever it was had been butchered and it wasn't the first murder in Woodland Creek in that fashion.

There was a good chance the body was that of Jude since the murders continued—were continuing—after his disappearance. But, was Jude Mina's father? The Thomas family was one of the founding families and still had strong ties to the community. I had to be careful how I poked my nose around, being an outsider and all.

"What you doing?" Zeke peered over my shoulder as I closed the file. "Why you so obsessed with that tramp?"

Growling, I spit out, "She's no tramp." Zeke put his hands up and sat down across from me. "Leave her be, Zeke. I mean it."

"She's our target. Isn't that why we came here, to make sure the Spitz line was forever extinguished?" So he did know who she was. I should've known that mother would have told him, too. "I enjoy the cat and mouse game myself, but this has gone on long enough, Rollo. I want to go home."

Slamming my hands on the table I bellowed, "Then go. I'm not stopping you. I'm making sure all the facts line up. I'll take care of her." I left it there because I didn't need him suspicious of my true intentions.

"Your dick is clouding your judgement, brother." He stood up and left the room.

Throwing all the papers to the floor, I clasped my head in my hands. Victoria tried telling me that Mina probably had something to do with Scott's death, but I knew otherwise. Mina wasn't a murderer. Fifteen years ago Jude and Mora had been rumored to be dating, but Mora was also close with my uncle Scott. Jesus. I was probably digging up some horrid love triangle and there was no telling what I'd find. Hell, maybe Scott had killed them both. And it still didn't explain why Victoria was involved.

Taking my chances, I packed everything up and headed to the Thomas estate. Jillian Thomas, the matriarch, was still alive and I hoped she'd be willing to talk to me.

I pulled up the long tree-lined drive and took in the huge Victorian home. It needed some work, but was classically beautiful. I was invited into the house, but my guard was up. The house reeked of cats and could've qualified for an episode of Hoarders. Following the young girl to the back of the house, the clutter disappeared and I was escorted into a formal living room with antique furniture. Aware of my size, I didn't dare sit down on the delicate furniture.

There was a ruckus coming from another hallway as I heard an old lady bicker with another woman. "Who let the dog in? I can smell him all the way on the other side of the house." The old lady walked into the room and took in my figure. I could only assume that the 'dog' she was referring to was me. The rumors appearing to be true that they were in deed wizards. "Well, aren't you quite the specimen." Funny how her demeanor changed as she scoured my body.

"Mrs. Thomas I presume, Rollo Frost."

I tried to stretch out my hand, but she'd already turned to take her seat. She wasn't even done positioning herself when a cat jumped into her lap and hissed at me.

"Calm down, Skittles." She stroked the cat and ordered me to sit. "It can hold you, now sit down." I did as she instructed and waited. "So, Rollo Frost.

What can I do for you?"

"Well, there's no point in beating around the bush. I'm here about your son, Jude, and his connection to Mora Spitz."

"Eck, she was a filthy dog; quite a piece of work. Men falling at her feet and all she did was string them all along." Leering at me, "If I remember correctly, your uncle was one of them."

"I wouldn't know, Ma'am. That's why I'm here. I'm trying to find out what really happened to them, all of them."

She studied me with her eyes, "No, there's more. If you can't be truthful, then don't expect any help from me."

Puffing out a breath, I ran my hands over my beard. "I'm trying to help a friend uncover the identity of her father. Mina Spitz." Her eyes didn't waver from my face and I continued. "I believe that Jude may be her father."

"Pah! Not a chance. Mora came to town with that child on her hip. My Jude would've claimed his child."

"That may be, but what if he didn't know?" That

seemed to get her attention. "My pack banished Mora and her baby, rumors circulating about rape or cheating." I could see her turning red. "I'm not saying your son raped her. I believe there's more to the story. But, Mina is my primary concern."

"That girl was nothing but a delinquent as a teenager, probably still is." I smiled at that. Mina had been in and out of trouble as a teenager, but all minor offenses.

"Something is brewing inside her, causing blackouts, and I think you might know what it is. It's more than shifter inside her. There's magic in her."

Narrowing her eyes at me, she pursed her lips at me before speaking. "If what you're saying is true, why isn't Mina here herself?"

"Honestly, she doesn't know I'm here. I think she's convinced Jude murdered her mother and never looked further than that."

"You care for her." I dropped my eyes as she added, "You're keeping secrets from her and they're going to get someone killed."

"That's what I'm worried about. Her powers are

growing..."

"What powers? Thomas powers are unique."

"I think they're weather related. When she's angry or scared is when I notice it most, like a storm cloud following her.   But the blackouts come after she's shifted."

"AMY! Get me the book." She looked at me and warned, "If what you speak is truth, I may agree with you, but be careful. She needs to be brought here so we can work with her before someone is seriously hurt. Her powers are fighting for control with each other. She needs help."   Amy returned to the room and handed Jillian a book as she shoved the cat off Jillian's lap who then moved to sit next to me. "I'll need Mina, or something of hers to confirm she's who you think she is."

"I don't know that she'll agree to that."

"You find a way. A drop of blood, strand of hair, either will let me identify if she's part of my bloodline. We need to start there."

She opened the book and began talking to me and showing me things that enlightened and scared me.

The power that Mina seemed to have was one that skipped generations and only resided in the women. It was even rarer for Mina to have it since she was technically a half-breed. Then Jillian showed me news clippings from some horrific storms that had obliterated small towns in the Midwest. She informed me that they were caused by women with similar powers who'd never learned to control them.

She confirmed that they hadn't seen Jude since the night Mora was murdered. "My boy is gone, has been since that night, but I didn't feel his loss until a few months ago. I would know if he was still alive. Do you know when these blackouts started with her?"

"A few months ago, I think. After my uncle Scott died."

Shaking her head, "This doesn't make any sense. IF Jude was her father he could've withheld her power to help teach her how to control it. Only a parent can do that, a living parent. But you said she didn't start having the blackouts until recently." She stood up and paced the room and began talking to herself. "Jude was always playing tricks on people." She looked to me. "I need to do some of my own research."

She pulled me to my feet and started walking me to the door. She knew something, but wasn't revealing it. "Mrs. Thomas, if you know something..."

"If you notice it most when she's angry or scared, she most certainly isn't fully aware or she's in denial. The blackouts are happening because she hasn't learned to control it. When I find out more, I'll be in touch."

She handed me a piece of paper and I wrote my number down for her before she shoved me out the door. I stood there, the door nearly hitting my face and tried to process everything she'd told me. How was it in a couple hours I'd been able to find out more than Mina had in years of searching? She'd admitted to me that she'd never gone down the Thomas path because she was convinced Jude either murdered her mother, or had been murdered himself. She never suspected he could be her father.

I wasn't even aware that I was driving to Mina's until I pulled down her street. Her truck wasn't in the drive so I risked it and pulled up in front of her house. I knocked on the front door and then walked around to the back. I was surprised to see a note addressed to 'Red' on the table.

Grabbing the letter, I put it in my pocket and left. Pulling down a dirt road close to home, I parked my uncle's truck, which I'd commandeered as mine, and pulled out the note.

Dear Red,

> *I fear that your feelings for me are unwarranted. I don't deserve your kindness. I've betrayed you, myself, and another. I made a mistake and I don't know how to fix it. How I wish you'd shown yourself to me and maybe this could've been avoided.*
>
> *I've been alone for so long, maybe I'm better off that way. I mishandled everything. Now I'm torn between the two of you. You both fill my dreams. I'm a mess and don't know how to fix it.*
>
> *I understand if you wash your hands of me. I'd probably do the same. All I've ever wanted is a pack of my own. I can't deny the security I feel when you're around. You know more about me than any other person and that scares me to death.*
>
> *I hope you come back around, but I understand if you don't.*

Sincerely,
Mina

She was torturing herself that was for sure. I had to see her and confess. I couldn't let her continue to beat herself up when the two people she was torn between were one in the same. I headed back into town and found her truck parked behind her shop. It was now or never.

MINA

I spent a lot of time in the shop and at home the days following my rendezvous with Rollo. I couldn't be at home and not think of Red and when I went to the shop all I could envision was Rollo and I on the massage table. I dove into inventory reports and going over the books, reorganizing the shelves, and deep cleaning. Anything to try to keep my mind off of them both.

The bell rang and I looked up from where I was sitting at the counter and saw him stroll in. Why was he here? His eyes locked on mine before he checked to see if anyone else was in the shop. When he realized what I already knew, that we were alone, he marched over to me, only the counter separating us. I put on a brave face and smiled.

"Can I help you?"

"Is that how it's going to be?" He stared at me and I couldn't look him in the eyes. I was so conflicted. No one had ever affected me so. "I wanted to apologize."

What? "What!?"

"Don't seem so surprised, Mina. I didn't mean for things to go down the way they did between us."

"How did you plan for them to go down? I told you I was only willing to give you one night."

"Dammit, Mina." He turned around and began pacing the floor. "Is this really who you are? Was I *that* off base with you? Random hookups and one-night stands."

I stared back at him as one song ended and another began. I couldn't work without music playing, it was something I let distract me. *Rescue My Heart* by Liz Longley started playing as I tried finding words for Rollo. "Are you trying to tell me that you're really any different?"

Slamming his hands on the counter, he sneered at me. "Don't judge a book by its cover, Mina. I *am* very different and I don't just take anyone to my bed."

"Well, you haven't taken me to your bed either."

"You think I let any hussy ride my face?"

Standing, I slammed my own hands on the counter. "I'm not a HUSSY!" Thunder cracked and I could feel the temperature change. I pinched the bridge of my nose before sitting back down on the stool.

"Mina, I didn't come here to fight. I came here about this." He motioned to the window and the sound of hail pelting the windows. "I can help."

Shaking my head and feeling completely defeated, I revealed my fear. "You can't help. No one can. I don't know what's going on with me."

"What if I told you I knew someone who could help?"

Looking in his eyes, I confessed, "I'd tell you that I'm scared. Shifters are disappearing. How do I know you're not the one responsible?"

"Shifters?"

Rolling my eyes, "Don't pretend you don't know. We both know what we are."

He nodded, "I know. So, what's your shifter form?"

I shook my head. "I don't trust you that much. Not

yet. Prove to me that I can trust you first."

"Ok. I get that. Let me be your friend, Mina."

Friend? Could I be *just* friends with Rollo? "You don't want to be just my friend, Rollo."

Grinning, he agreed. "True. But I can try."

I wasn't sure, but I knew I didn't want to walk away from him completely either. I'd rather have him for a friend, than nothing at all. I stuck my hand out, "Friends."

"Deal."

"Now, you said you know someone who could help?"

"Yes, but you're not going to be happy about it." I narrowed my eyes at him and he continued on. "It's Jillian Thomas."

"Absolutely not!"

"Mina, her son didn't kill your mother."

I took a step back from him knowing I hadn't revealed that suspicion to him. "How do you know that?" I was growing suspicious.

"Mina, it's not what you think. Scott told me more than I let on. I should've told you. I'm sorry."

"But you said…"

"Fuck what I said. I didn't want you to think I was some stalker. I promise, I just want to help."

Crossing my arms over my chest I asked, "What makes you so certain Jude Thomas didn't kill my mother?"

Exhaling sharply, his admission shocked me. "Because I believe Jude Thomas is your father."

I shook my head, sure confusion resided in my expression. "No. There's no way. That makes no sense." Hail began pelting the windows again as blinding light penetrated my vision. Pinching the bridge of my nose, I exhaled sharply. "Rollo, there's something you don't know."

"What is it?"

"I've been having blackouts, but they usually only happen after I shift. I need to go home." My vision was spotty and my head was pounding. I tried standing, but couldn't manage it. "Please, take me home before I blackout again."

He scooped me in his arms and said, "The hell I'm taking you home. We're going to see Jillian."

"No! Please. It'll pass in a few hours. Then I'll go with you to see Jillian." His eyes came into focus and he begrudgingly conceded.

"Fine. But I'm not happy about it."

I vaguely remember giving him the security code for my alarm system and then him carrying me up to my bedroom. He put me in bed and then everything went black. When I rolled over several hours later, it was to see it was the middle of the night.

"Rollo?" Just when I thought that maybe he'd left me alone, I heard him walk into the room. He was shirtless as his large frame filled the doorway while he rubbed at his eyes. "Sorry, didn't mean to wake you."

"It's fine. Everything ok?"

"Yeah, for now anyway."

"I took the room next door. I hope that's ok."

I nodded, "Yeah, its fine. You can head home if you want."

He just shook his head. "Nope, we're going to see Jillian. You're not getting out of it. But I am going to sleep for a few more hours, maybe go for a run."

Yawning, I laid back down. "Knock yourself out."

He stood over me and brushed some hair from my temple. "Get some rest, Mina."

"You, too." Being friends fucking sucked.

Later that morning we were headed to the Thomas estate. I couldn't stop playing with my hair. It was a nervous habit that Rollo was picking up on.

"You'll be fine. I won't let anything happen to you."

We walked into a house that was cluttered and filled with cats. Each one we passed hissed at us as we snickered. Fucking cat people. Rollo sat down next to me on an antique couch and grabbed my hand, giving it a reassuring squeeze before releasing it.

"So you're Mina." I bolted to my feet, not sure what to expect. She stared at me and I was growing increasingly more nervous. "You're the spitting image of your mother, though her eyes weren't blue if I recall correctly."

"No, yes. You're correct. Her eyes were brown." I noted that Jillian's eyes were blue, as well as the girl who stood beside her.

"Jude's eyes were blue, like yours."

I shook my head and looked away. "I'm sorry. This is just a lot to take in. I don't know that I believe he's my father."

"Well, that's what we're going to find out." She patted my cheek and then told me to sit down. She grabbed something off a tray and poked my finger with it before I could react.

"Ow!" I yanked my hand away and stuck the pricked tip in my mouth. "What the hell was that?"

"My own special DNA test. With magic of course." She headed toward the door and announced, "Blood works faster. I'll be back shortly."

Once she was gone, I glared at Rollo. "What the hell, dude?"

Grinning, "Dude? Really?"

"This isn't funny, Rollo."

Trying to give me a straight face, he apologized. "I'm sorry. I know it's not funny, but it was just a finger poke."

"You could've warned me."

Jillian walked back into the room. "Stand up dear." I did as she asked. Clutching my cheeks, she examined my face. "I never would've suspected, but those eyes. They're my Jude's eyes."

My stomach dropped as her words sank in. "So, you mean…"

"You're my grand-daughter." She clasped me to her and I didn't know if I should hug her back or push her off of me. She pushed me to arm's length and said, "Shifter, huh? That might be a first in our family tree."

I stumbled back to the couch and sat down heavily. Rollo's hand gently ran across my back, trying to comfort me. I was aware of Jillian speaking to the young woman, but couldn't make out anything they were saying. My brain was in overdrive and the boom of thunder that followed got everyone's attention.

Jillian grew silent and stepped closer to me. She gently raised my face with her soft, wrinkled hands. "Do you even know what you're capable of?" Thunder rumbled again as I got the confirmation I'd so desperately been seeking. "You're doing this. The weather has been acting up for a few months now and now we know the reason why. Have you figured out how to control it?"

I shook my head, "No and if I shift when it happens, I black out."

"Yes. Both magic forces are competing for control. You need to figure out how to control it. It's a little different for everyone."

Stress filled my voice when I asked, "Why is this happening just now? I don't understand."

"That, my dear, we're trying to figure out. Only a blood parent can withhold your powers, Jude, but..."

"He's been dead for years."

"Or so we thought." She pulled up a chair and sat in front of me. "Jude was especially good at disguising himself, taking on the appearance of others. That was his magic specialty."

"What? I don't understand."

She sighed, "I have a sneaking suspicion that who you all believed to be Scott Frost, was truly my Jude. He would've gone to any length to protect his own. Even if that meant living in secrecy."

Rollo interjected, "If Jude was disguised as my Uncle Scott, then where's my uncle?"

Jillian shrugged her shoulders, "That's what we

need to figure out. There's no telling if he's alive or in hiding."

I started crying, "So, you think that Scott was really Jude? All those years I was with my father and I had no idea." Pulling my knees up, I curled into myself. Every memory of Scott, or Jude, whomever it was, ran through my brain. Storms brewed internally and outside.

I heard Rollo talking and then Jillian telling him to stay back. "I want to see something. Mina, look at me." I did as she asked. "I want you to let the emotions take over, just for a moment."

"Is that safe?"

"Hush, boy."

"Were you there the night your mother was killed?" It was as if she was trying to anger me.

Before I knew it, the room became dim as the sun was suddenly drowned out with black clouds. The lights flickered as I became more and more upset. So many secrets. Why had my father kept them from me, if he was truly my father? He had so many opportunities to reveal himself to me and I would've kept the secret. I would've let him adopt me. My vision shifted as I stood, taking deep breaths. Glass smashed and a violent breeze filled the room.

"The eyes! Mina, you have to learn to control it."

I didn't want to control it. I wanted to succumb to the power, let it consume me and take me over. I could feel the power surging through me, like an adrenaline high, and I wanted more. Closing my eyes, my arms stretched out as I smiled at the toxicity of the feelings running through my body.

"Rollo, she has to be stopped!"

ROLLO

I stood back in amazement, knowing I should probably be fearful of what I was watching. Mina's eyes were aglow, like lanterns in the night, as a storm outside began to catapult the house.

Jillian looked to me assuming I was the key and

bellowed, "Rollo, she has to be stopped!" I don't know what she thought I could possibly do and the expression I flashed at her told her so. "Are you in love with her? Only a lover has the power to reach her now. You must try."

"How?" How did she know how I felt about Mina? I wasn't even sure I believed it myself. It was too soon and Mina didn't even know, not that I knew of. And we weren't exactly lovers.

"That's what you need to figure out. If you don't try, we'll have to use our own measures to get her to stop."

I took another step toward Mina and reached out to touch her, but ceased as doubt filled me. I wasn't even sure if she could hear me or see me. Where did I even start? Did I try to touch her, talk to her? I had no idea. My powers of persuasion never seemed to work on her, so what use would they do me now?

Stepping in front of her, I tried making eye contact with her. "Mina, you have to control it." Something crashed against the outside of the house and I moved closer to her. Taking her hand, I let my eyes shift and willed her to hear my thoughts. *"Mina, please stop. Focus on me. You're safe, I'll keep you safe."*

Her hand squeezed mine back and her eyes blinked. Slowly the glow of her eyes subsided. When I was convinced she was fully out of it I let my eyes return to their human likeness and then she collapsed in my arms.

Jillian directed us to the couch, "That much power, when you're not used to it, is exhausting. Let her rest." I placed her on the small couch and knelt by her. "Does she know?"

I knew what Jillian had to be referring to. "If she does, she refuses to acknowledge it."

"It's the magic. Deep down she knows or you wouldn't have been able to get through to her just now. Keep trying. You two have a bond, believe that."

We agreed that Mina should go home, but that I needed to stay close to her. She was barely coherent when I laid her in her bed.

The next few days she kept very quiet, but went to see Jillian every day to learn more about her powers. Mentally, Mina seemed to push me away, yet her demeanor was calmer and she didn't object to me being around. I wasn't sure if she was shutting down or discovering the possibilities.

When I got to her place that night, she was nowhere to be found, but her truck was parked in the drive. My senses told me that she'd gone for a run. She was gaining a little more control over her powers, but Jillian had warned her to tread lightly. Walking into the woods behind her house, I disrobed and inhaled deeply, picking up her scent almost immediately. Shifting, I then took off in pursuit of her.

I found her on our hill, my true identity still a secret to her, or she was playing me for a fool. She let me know that she was aware of my presence and whimpered softly as I stalked toward her. My need for her was most overpowering in our shifter forms. Nose to nose, we circled one another. I nipped at her neck and she showed her fangs and nipped back. We played this game for several moments before she took off running.

Following behind, when I caught up to her I jumped on her as we wrestled with each other. Managing to get out from under me, she stood and faced me. Then slowly, she turned and surrendered. Nuzzling her, she returned the gesture. Mounting her was the only thing left to do and that's just what I did.

She willingly granted me the access I so desperately craved. I couldn't hide myself from her any longer. Once we were done, I would reveal myself to her and pray she didn't run from me or try to kill me. No matter what mission my stepmother had sent me on, I would never follow through with it. Mina was now my top priority to protect instead of extinguish. She was mine.

As the tremors began to fill me, I bit at the scruff of her neck as she whimpered. We fell to the ground once I'd spent myself. With her back nestled to my chest, she shifted back to her human form. She didn't turn to look at me and in the darkness we could barely make each other out. I, too, shifted back.

Wrapping my arms around her, she panted, "Finally. Red…" She stopped before finishing her train of thought.

Taking a deep breath, because I knew the fight that was about to commence, I whispered her name.

"Mina." She cooed and relaxed and just as quick bolted out of my arms and turned to look at me, recognizing my voice. "Mina, please let me explain."

"It's you? You're Red?" Shaking her head, she questioned me, "Why didn't you tell me?" I stood up and made a move toward her which she rejected. "No, don't come any closer."

"Mina, please relax. Listen to your instincts. We're bonded and the magic from your father is tarnishing your shifter side."

She gaped at me. "I'm not tarnished."

"That's not what I meant. Even you have confided in me and in Red that your shifter senses are all out of whack. Well, mine aren't."

"I, you, you were supposed to be my friend."

"Mina, I am. But I can't deny what's here between us."

Turning away, she said, "I need time to process this. Please don't follow me."

Before I could object, she ran off. If she thought I wasn't going to follow her, she was out of her mind. I stayed far enough back that she couldn't see me, but I never let her out of my sight. Surprisingly, no storm brewed overhead and I wondered what that meant. Was she finally gaining control of her powers?

She walked up the steps of her deck and shifted. Looking into the woods, she made eye contact with me before heading back inside. I lay down on the property line, like a watchdog and waited.

Some time passed, maybe an hour, and I was getting dressed when I heard her patio door slide open again. As I zipped my pants, my eyes darted to her back deck.

"Rollo!" Her tone didn't suggest that this would be a friendly conversation.

I grabbed the remainder of my clothes and walked toward her. She wore leggings and a baggy t-shirt with no bra, her nipples poking through the shirt a tell-tale sign. I stood a few feet back as she took a deep breath. I could hear music blaring inside, but wasn't focused on it. All of my attention was on her.

"So, you've known about me for how long?"

Narrowing my eyes, I asked, "Known what? Who you are, that you're a shifter, the connection to my uncle? I'm not sure what you're asking, Mina."

Huffing, she raised her voice. "All of it! How could you lead me on all these weeks? Running around here, letting me spill all my secrets to you." I took a step closer, seeing she was getting overly agitated. "How could you do that to me? You're a coward."

"You're right. I was scared. You were the last thing I expected to find when I came to town."

"Somehow I don't believe that."

She was partially right. "I know the magic has muddled your senses, but mine are as keen as ever." I stepped in front of her and she stopped pacing. Her chin was downcast and she was twiddling her thumbs, trying to keep her hands busy. "Look at me, Mina."

"Please don't make me look at you." It was a plea and I wasn't sure what she was getting at.

"Mina, why don't you want to look at me? I've kept your secrets, protected you, and been your friend and confidant. All I want is you." She took in a shaky breath as I asked again, "Please look at me, Mina."

She raised her gorgeous blue eyes to mine and floored me with her actions. Wrapping her arms around my neck, she pulled my mouth down to hers. Lifting her without hesitation, she wrapped her legs around me as I held her easily against me.

Her teeth pulled on my upper lip causing me to growl in response. I walked into the kitchen with her body clinging to mine and slid the door shut. Setting her ass on the kitchen table, she pulled me down on top of her. Bracing my arm on the table, I broke the kiss as we both stared at the other.

"Mina. There's no going back..."

"I want to be owned by you in ways I didn't know possible...until now. Rollo, please. I'm sorry I fought it." I was shocked silent at her words. "I need you in my life."

"I plan on doing more than owning you. I'm going to fucking brand you."

Carrying her up the stairs, I threw her on the bed and began unbuttoning my pants. The remainder of my clothes that I'd been holding had been discarded once she'd kissed me on the deck. The music that was filling the house was coming from her room. The unique sounds of *Infinity* by The xx filled the room. Stopping before I pulled my pants down, I sat down on the bed and motioned for her to come closer.

Pulling her over my lap, she didn't fight me. "Have you ever been spanked, Mina? Truly spanked?"

"What, I... No."

"Relax."

I gently rubbed circles over the curve of her ass after pushing her shirt up. Kneading her, I waited until I felt her relax and then unleashed the first whack of my hand.

"Oh!"

I just smiled and struck one cheek after the other as she melted into my lap. "How's that feel, Mina?"

"Wh, what?"

Chuckling, I repeated the question. "How does it feel?"

"Good. Really good."

Pulling her leggings down, I found her wearing no panties. My handprints were the only thing her ass wore. Running my hands all over them before I trailed my finger down the seam of her ass and into her pussy. She was wet, but I wanted her wetter. A small moan of protest left her lips when my fingers removed themselves. Resuming my previous task, I began smacking her ass once again.

"Rollo!" It was a plea for more.

Ceasing, I pulled her up. "Come here." Now on her knees, straddling my thigh, I cupped her face as her heavy eyes closed fully. Kissing her, I reached an arm between her legs. She sat on my upper forearm while my hand squeezed her ass.

The gasps that left her lips were intoxicating and sounds that I'd not soon forget. Laying her down, I pushed her shirt up and exposed her smooth nipples to the cool air, watching them bud up. Her hands gripped the comforter as I kissed down her torso. The closer my mouth got between her legs the higher her back arched off the bed.

I found her dripping and couldn't resist tasting her. I still hadn't forgotten her flavor from that night all those weeks ago, but needed to experience it again. I got comfortable and let my tongue drag over her from bottom to top and back again. Cooing my name, she rocked her hips to the motion of my mouth as I continued to lick and suck her.

Lifting my head, I pushed a finger inside and quickly followed with a second as I watched her eyes flutter shut. Easing in a third, to prepare her for me, she moaned devilishly. Kissing her clit until she gasped, I then pulled away. Standing next to the bed, she quickly rose to her knees and ran her hands over my chest and arms.

Reaching into my pants, her eyes found mine after she wrapped her delicate hand around my throbbing girth. Cupping her chin, I kissed her as my hands moved into her hair while she stroked me. Her free hand pushed my pants from my hips until they fell to the floor. Stepping free of them, I climbed onto the bed gently pushing her back down. We kissed and touched for some time. I wanted her desperate and on the edge when I took her.

"Rollo, please don't make me beg."

Smiling against her neck, I retorted, "That's exactly what I plan on doing."

"Please, Rollo..." She found my cock and stroked him until I moaned, eyes slamming shut at the sensation.

Kneeling between her legs, I took in her beauty once again. Her body shimmered with the heat of us as her slightly parted lips pressed closed as she tried to catch her breath.

"You're mine now, Mina. You understand me?"

Nodding, she whimpered her approval. "I'm yours."

Slowly, I guided my throbbing dick into her waiting pussy. I took my time, making sure I didn't hurt her. Once she took all of me, I kissed her lips before pulling out and sliding back in, but faster.

"Oh, God."

Her breath caught over and over again as we began to move as one. Fingernails clung to my biceps as sweat trickled down between my shoulders. Lowering my head, I sucked and nipped on her neck as she panted in my ear, begging for more.

"I feel it Rollo. It's true what you said." I looked to her eyes to find them slightly aglow and pushed in harder. "You're mine as much as I am yours. Ahh!"

She threw her head back as I let go and gave her

everything I had. I saw tears begin to fill her eyes as she continued gasping. It wasn't uncommon for some to be moved so emotionally when a connection had been found. Her threatening tears filled me with a joy that I wasn't sure how to contain.

"Let go, Mina. Let it happen."

A few moments later, she cried out, thrashing against me and the bed as thunder boomed outside. Now that was something I could get used to, as long as she could control it. Nothing like knowing you've moved the heavens with the orgasm you've given her.

"Mina, I can't wait much longer."

Pulling my mouth to hers, she panted, "Then don't wait. Let it happen, Rollo." She kissed me and then her words became my undoing. "I want my name to be the growl that falls from your lips, branding my soul as your release floods me."

Her eyes locked with mine and that's exactly what happened. "Mina!"

It was probably the most intimate moment I'd ever had with another being. Collapsing on top of her, I rolled to my side and brought her with me where we both passed out from exhaustion.

MINA

So, people talk about mind blowing sex and I thought I knew what they meant, but I was mistaken. What I experienced with Rollo was indescribable. I was still floating on a high as I stepped out of the shower. As I ran the towel over my body, my ass felt tender to the touch so I turned to look in the mirror. I was surprised to see bruises forming all over my ass. I know he gave me quite the spanking—that I rather enjoyed—but had no idea he'd marked me so.

He came strolling into the bathroom, sleep still clouding his eyes. "What the hell, Rollo?" He stopped dead in his tracks and followed the motion of my hand. "You marked me!" I was trying to sound mad, but it was quite humorous knowing that I enjoyed every minute of it.

Stalking over to me, a grin covered his face as he replied, "I told you I was going to brand you. Consider those bruises the first marks of my ownership."

"First marks? Who says I'll let you do it again?"

Laughing, he said, "Honey, you loved it as much as I did. No point in denying it. But right now, I'm going to thoroughly enjoy you in many forms of movements and positions."

My jaw dropped. Usually I could throw the banter right back, but he left me speechless. I just shook my head at him as he stalked closer and wrapped his arms around me. He turned the shower back on and dragged me in with him, not that I objected.

We spent most of the day naked and christening every room of my house. We were lounging on the couch that night when he suggested we go out for dinner. I was famished and hadn't grocery shopped in days, so I agreed. We walked into the local diner and all eyes couldn't help but fall on his enormous figure. He had a presence that I'd grown so accustomed to, I forgot how others reacted to it. Some looked twice at seeing me on his arm and others couldn't care less.

We were almost done with our meal when two voices I recognized ran like nails down a chalkboard on my senses. This was going to get very interesting very quickly. Zeke, Dixie, and some others I didn't know by name headed straight for us. Rollo gave my leg a reassuring squeeze as they gathered to stand in front of us.

"Where've you been, man?" Zeke's question had me calculating how much time Rollo had been spending with me and it was quite significant. But he was also a grown adult.

"Around. Is there something you need?"

Zeke's cold brown eyes looked to me and back to Rollo's. "Can we talk alone?"

"Nope. I'm busy. If you have something to say, you can say it in front of her." Rollo's challenge wasn't lost on me.

I was growing uncomfortable and started to slide out of the booth. "I can give you a few."

Rollo gripped my wrist, demanding, "Stay." I knew his anger wasn't directed at me, but couldn't help but wonder what the issue was. "Zeke, out with it or leave."

Zeke growled and Rollo jumped to his feet as the two came nose to chin, Rollo having the advantage. Zeke stepped back, grabbed Dixie's arm and bellowed, "This isn't going to fly, Rollo."

Rollo ignored him as everyone who followed Zeke into the diner walked right back out with him. Reclaiming his seat next to me, I finished my meal in silence. I was curious what the big debate was—cuz clearly there was one—and had a pretty good feeling it had something to do with me. And that was something Rollo would tell me if he needed to, or so I convinced myself.

That night when we got back to my place, he didn't walk in with me. "I should go chat with Zeke. I've neglected my pack and I need to set some things straight."

Nodding, I agreed. I didn't want to pry, but made sure he knew he had my support. "If there's anything I can do to help... Please let me know."

Smiling, he kissed my forehead. "Thank you. You'll

.M. Witt

be ok alone?"

"Yes. Don't see why not."

"Ok. I'll call you tomorrow."

"I'll be at the shop most of the day. And you have the code if you change your mind."

Slapping my ass, he kissed me before walking back down the drive and to his truck. I watched as he pulled away before closing the door and setting the alarm. I sat down on the couch and realized just how tired I was. Dragging myself up the stairs, I removed all my clothing and climbed into my bed that had his scent bathed all over it. I slept like a baby that night.

I woke a few hours later thinking of him. There was no more denying it. I craved his touch more than I craved the freedom of the run. I wanted to feel him all over me, to get lost in him, lost in us. And it was more than his touch, it was his company, his presence. When I was with him, all my problems seemed to dissipate and I remembered that I was just a person seeking a connection with another human being. A connection that was all consuming, a connection that could only be felt with another person. Rollo was that connection.

I spread out under the covers reveling in the feel of them against my naked flesh. Rolling to my stomach, my hands ran over my ass and squeezed the tender bruises there. The only effect it had on me was to miss him more. I was already in deep and knew it.

My dreams were saturated with him. More than once I woke up squeezing my pillow and panting, feeling him there with me. How the hell was I going to get anything done if my thoughts were constantly on him?

The next day at the shop, he showed up with coffee almost as if he knew how tired I'd be. Smiling, I gladly accepted his gift of caffeine and continued about my tasks. My afternoon was full of appointments so I was busy making sure all my lotions and oils were fully stocked, linens clean and folded, and that everything was in its place.

"Busy day?"

Nodding, I confirmed, "Yes, three massages back to back." Looking up I inquired about his day. "What about you?"

Shrugging his shoulders, "Just the same old. I need

to visit some of Scott's clients and hope they want to continue with their snow removal service that he provided."

"I'm sure they will."

"Yeah, well. You're not the new guy in town. Everyone looks at me like I'm a stranger."

Smiling, "Because you are. You're pretty intimidating. Lighten up and I'm sure everything will be fine. And try to smile. That smile does wonders for you." I winked at him as he narrowed his eyes at me.

"You make it sound so easy."

"The people here are loyal. Prove to them that you're part of that, part of Scott's legacy. If you can do that, you're in. And, besides, there isn't anyone else in town offering snow removal."

He closed the distance between us. His arm snaked around my waist and cupped my ass, sending shivers up my spine, as he pulled me close. "Thanks for the tip." Leaning down, he softly pressed his lips to mine.

Heat immediately flooded my body as his tongue grazed mine, his hands roaming my body as mine gripped his triceps. "Rollo."

"Yes, Mina?"

Moaning, I pleaded with him. "We have to stop. My first client will be here any minute."

"What if I don't want to stop?" Before I could say anything, the bell from the door opening broke our reverie. "Hmm. We'll continue this later."

"Counting on it." We were in the back room, shielded from prying eyes, but I asked him to wait a minute while I went and greeted my client. Straightening my clothes, I put on a smile and greeted Lorraine. "Are you ready?"

"Yes. Should I just go ahead and go in?"

"Yup." I motioned her to the room. "It's all ready. I'll be in shortly."

Once she closed the door, Rollo emerged from the back room and squeezed my ass. I moaned as he whispered in my ear, "Still tender."

"Yes, in a good way." He swatted me once, hard, and then left. I had to take a few deep breaths to compose myself. Then I walked into the room where Lorraine waited. "How's that neck doing? Better I

J.M. Witt

hope."

That night when I headed outside, Rollo's truck was parked next to mine. He rolled down his window and smiled at me. I walked over and stepped up on the steps, leaning my head in his window.

"Waiting for someone?"

Pulling me close, he kissed me and it was all tongue. "Yup. I just found her."

"Mmm." I pulled his lips back to mine and reveled in the kiss before breaking it. "Did you want to go somewhere?"

"I thought you'd never ask."

Smiling, I climbed down and said, "Follow me."

I headed back to my place. Throwing some logs in the fireplace, Rollo lit it as I removed my shoes. Heading to the kitchen, I brewed some water wanting some hot chocolate. He walked up behind me and snaked his arms around me.

"You're not avoiding me are you?"

"Not in the least." Turning, I wrapped my arms around him, resting my head on his chest. "I just thought it'd be nice to sit in front of the fire and have some hot chocolate."

"I like the sound of that, too."

We curled up on the floor with our cups of hot cocoa and music playing. Sitting between his knees and resting my head against his chest, I felt so at peace. It'd been a crazy couple months, but everything happened for a reason, right?

I sighed louder than I thought I had because he questioned me. "You ok?"

"Hmm. Yes. Just thinking about the past several weeks and months."

"And?"

I just shrugged my shoulders. "Nothing. Just... Happy."

His finger came under my chin and tilted it back toward his face. Softly, he kissed me as he caressed my face. "Me, too."

He set his mug down on the table and then did the same with mine. Soon we were on the floor, tangled in one another. *Poison* by Vaults played as the heat from the fire had a slight sweat glistening on us both. And the shadows cast from the light were seductive. If we were each other's poison, I didn't want a cure.

Sitting naked on the floor, face to face with him, my legs and arms wrapped around him tight as I rode him. Both of us pulling on one another's hair while nipping and sucking at every inch of skin our mouths could reach.

"Mina..."

My eyes found his as the slow drum beat of the song helped us keep rhythm with one another. "Yes, Rollo?"

He hesitated, "I..."

"What is it?" I was nervous at the thought of what he may have wanted to say.

"I can't get enough of you."

Silly girl. Breathless, I returned the sentiment. "Likewise." He tugged on my hair violently, exposing my neck to his teeth as he scraped them over the delicate flesh. "Oh, don't stop, Rollo."

Rolling me to my back, he leaned up and gave me all he had. "Play with your pussy."

I did as he commanded and soon I was falling apart underneath him as he burrowed deep inside me, his own orgasm taking hold. Panting, we lay there for several moments before he rolled to his side and we fell asleep.

ROLLO

I woke a while later to find us sleeping on the floor. Helping her to her feet, we walked up the stairs and climbed into bed.

"Oh, the sheets are cold." Laughing, I pulled her close. Sighing, "You're so warm. I don't want to freeze you out."

"You're fine. Come here."

Wrapping my body around hers, we lay face to face. Kissing every inch of her face, she sighed in contentment. How quickly she'd become more precious to me than any other thing or person ever had. Rolling, she turned her back to me and nuzzled closer into me. My hands traced her hip as she cooed in response. Pressing back against me, my need for her renewed.

"Mina..."

Sighing, she whispered, "Take me, Rollo."

Lifting her leg slightly, she gasped as I slid into her from behind. Reaching around, I cupped her as she clutched to my forearm. Firmly, I pressed my finger to her clit and the more pressure I applied, the more she squirmed and responded to me. She was lax against me and the look of pure ecstasy was on her face.

Pulling out of her, I yanked her ass to the edge of the bed and got on my knees in front of her. Wasting no time, I plunged two fingers into her wet pussy, and began licking her sweet nub. Immediately she began clenching around me as her gasps and moans became more prevalent. Moving my fingers back and forth I looked up to find her watching me. Groaning, her head dropped back down as she pushed harder into my hand.

"Come for me, Mina."

"Oh, God...Rollo." Her hands clutched the bedspread as she cried out, "Don't stop. I'm going to come... Oh..."

I had no intention of stopping, not until she pried my head away from her. And that's pretty much what happened. Climbing over her body, I kissed her before lying down next to her. Her energy restored, she crawled over me and knelt between my legs.

Without hesitation and a smile on her face she took me in her hand and licked me from root to tip. Tension released from my shoulders as I sank deeper into the bed reveling in the feel of her expert mouth.

"Christ, Mina."

Soon she increased the pressure of her sucking and I flooded her mouth shortly after. She didn't stop licking me until every drop was gone. With smiles on our faces, she curled into my side. Pulling her face to mine, I kissed her tenderly.

"Someone teach you that or are you a natural?"

Giggling, she replied, "I could ask you the same thing." When I didn't say anything she added, "I'd say I'm a natural. Enjoyed it did you?"

I simply grunted and pulled the covers over our bodies.

In the morning I was dressing when she began to stir. Smiling down and her, I kissed her lips after sitting down next to her.

"Don't go."

"I'll be back. I have some things to take care of. You have any plans for today?"

Shaking her head gently, she replied, "I'll probably go see Jillian, grandma—I don't know what to call her. Is that weird?"

"No. You're a grown woman and she just came into your life. I don't think anyone has expectations of you calling her grandma." I kissed her nose and stood back up. "I'll call you later."

"Mk. Be good."

I just smirked at her as she burrowed back under the covers. I wanted to stay there with her, but I had things to take care of. Victoria would be back in town soon and I had to find a way to stop all this madness with her and her obsession with Mina.

When I got back to the house, everyone was still sleeping. Lazy fuckers. They were all eager to go home once this was over. We'd discussed the plan before coming to Woodland Creek, but that was before *her*. Go to Woodland Creek, get rid of Mina, sell Scott's property, and then leave. Mina wasn't the only thing I wasn't expecting. Woodland Creek was the other. I was falling in love with this town and felt a peace here.

Falling in love. Fuck. Was I in love with Mina? I had to presume that I was. I'd never felt anything like it before. My father had always said to me, 'Son, with your mother I struggled living with her, but knew I didn't want to live without her. Unfortunately she was taken from us both too soon. But I wouldn't trade a single day of my life with her; good or bad.'

Even on his death bed my father whispered her name. Victoria was infuriated, though she tried to hide it. I felt sorry for Victoria. As much as she tried to fill the void my mother had left, she just couldn't do it. That was it. I was in love with Mina. Nothing and no one would ever fill me up the way she did.

"You're up." Turning, Zeke was standing in the garage doorway as I worked on one of the trucks.

"Yup. What's going on?"

"I could ask you the same thing. Pack is wondering

what's going on with you. We came here on a mission."

Dropping the tools into the toolbox, the loud clanking ringing in my ears, I wiped my hands on a rag. "Zeke. What aren't you telling me?" He just stared blankly at me. "Why does your mother want her dead? I need to know."

"You don't need to know. Tell me now if you can't handle it and I will."

Stepping closer to him, I got in his face, "You'll do no such thing. When is she getting here?"

He knew who I was referring to and replied, "In a few days."

"Nothing, and I mean NOTHING happens to Mina until I've spoken with Victoria. You understand me?"

He nodded and I stormed out of the garage. I drove into town and met with my PI again. He still didn't have anything new. I began to realize that it might be time to come up with a new plan, but that meant I'd have to tell Mina the truth. And that was something I didn't want to do. It would pretty much guarantee that I would lose her. And I couldn't blame her.

The PI was helpful and gave me some contacts to get fake IDs and some possible places Mina and I could run off to. If I couldn't talk Victoria down, I'd have no other option but to get Mina out of town. And there was no way I wasn't going with her, even if she hated me in the end.

When I got to Jillian's later that day, she and Mina were out in the back yard. Mina was entranced, eyes aglow, but she was doing things I hadn't yet seen or heard of her doing. Snowballs hovered in the air around her and before I knew it, one landed square in my chest. Laughing, I brushed the snow off before it soaked through.

Clapping, I praised her, "Well done. Since when did you gain the power of telekinesis?" She smiled, but she was still spellbound.

Jillian chimed in, "She's very special. She's come such a long way in such a short time. But it also makes her more dangerous and more vulnerable." She took a few steps toward me and lowered her voice. "If someone knows how potent her powers are, they may try to steal them."

"Steal them? You can do that?" She just nodded. "Fuck." She tilted her head at me in question. "It's nothing. I just had no idea."

"She's unique. Since she's half shifter and half wizard the odds were more likely that she'd have neither power. It's extremely rare that instead, she's twice as powerful, but twice as vulnerable to those who would want her power for the wrong reasons." I tried to process it all as she continued. "Just think of the devastation Mina could inflict if she put her mind to it. Now, give that power to someone who truly has evil or misguided intentions."

She didn't need to say anymore. I more than understood. Victoria must know about all of Mina's powers and wanted them for herself, but why? How the hell had I gotten myself into this mess? Thank God for that letter from Scott or Jude, whomever it was, because without it I may have never thought twice about what Victoria had sent me here to do.

Mina stopped shortly after. Running over, she threw her arms around my neck with a huge grin on her face. Jillian went inside and gave us some privacy.

Leaning back, she kissed me and then stopped when she knew I wasn't into it like I should've been.

"What's wrong?"

Shaking my head, "Just a lot going on with the pack. They're eager to go home." She tensed immediately. "Calm down. The plan was never to stay here in Woodland Creek."

Pushing out of my arms, she clammed up and red began to spread up her neck. "I, so, you're leaving?"

"Stop and let me finish. That was the plan, but things change." I pulled her back to me and got nose to nose with her. "I want to stay. I don't want to lead the pack if the pack takes me away from you."

"But it's who you are."

"People change, Mina." She started to object, "Stop. This is my choice to make if I make it."

"I'd hate to see you give up something so precious just for me."

"Don't you get it? You'd be the precious thing I can't give up, not the pack." She couldn't even make eye contact with me and I knew why. She didn't feel worthy, but that would change. One day she'd figure it out and I thoroughly looked forward to that day. Until then, I'd just keep showing her.

MINA

I was falling for him, hard, and now I was terrified he was going to leave. Maybe I should've offered to go with him. But his pack—most of them, anyway—hated me. I felt incredible guilt at the thought of him choosing me over them, but didn't know how to fix it.

Then it dawned on me. I should try to extend the olive branch and make amends with Zeke. I knew that he and Rollo had been raised as brothers and thought of each other that way. I had to try to get in Zeke's good graces. Anything to make it easier on Rollo. Of course, there was a chance it could make things worse, but I had to try.

Like a bad girlfriend, a few days later I snooped in Rollo's phone and copied down Zeke's phone number. I wasn't sure how else to get in touch with him without Rollo finding out. Now it was do or die. I sent him a text message and asked if he was willing to meet for a beer. I didn't take him as the coffee type, but I knew he liked beer.

I wasn't waiting as long for a response as I thought I'd have to wait. He accepted my invitation and we agreed to meet in the afternoon, knowing Rollo would be working in the garage. I smiled and hoped this helped. I really did want to make things easier for us all.

Sitting in Vider's, I waited for Zeke to show up. I hoped that he'd come alone, but I wasn't really sure if he would or not and it wasn't like I requested he did. But I assumed he knew it was implied.

Debi set a beer down in front of me and jerked her head toward the door. He was here. Taking a deep breath, I prepared myself as he sat down next to me. He ordered a beer and Debi brought it for him right away.

"So. You wanted to chat?"

Nodding, I set my beer down and turned to look at

him. "Thank you for meeting me. I know we got off on the wrong foot, Zeke. I'd like things to be amicable between us, for Rollo's sake."

I waited as he took a few sips of his beer, like he was contemplating what to say. "Took some gusto calling me. I know Rollo's been on edge, but clearly he's into you. I don't want to stand in the way of what he wants."

Wow. I was shocked he was being so cool about it all. Maybe I'd been wrong about him. We actually sat and talked about some of his childhood and how much trouble he and Rollo used to get into as kids. Sharing a few laughs, I became hopeful that Rollo wouldn't have to make a choice. He could have the pack and I both.

"I should head out. Got things to tend to."

"Ok. Thanks again, Zeke." He slapped down some money for the beers and I refused. "I got it."

"Nope. I believe I still owe you." He winked and again I was humbled. I just nodded and he took off.

"I still don't like him. He's shady." I turned to Debi as she glared at his figure walking out the door.

"I mean, he's kind of scummy, but we had a good

talk." I took a deep breath and let it out. "I really think everything's going to be fine."

Pursing her lips, she cautioned me, "Well, just be careful. I don't trust him."

Debi didn't trust anyone so I took her words with a grain of salt. "Yeah, yeah. I got it."

I left a while later and headed back to my shop. My phone alerted me of a text message and when I opened it up, it was from Zeke. Some of the words were jumbled, but they said that Rollo had been in an accident at the garage and that he needed me to come to Scott's immediately. I didn't hesitate. Locking up the shop, I jumped in my truck and high-tailed it to Rollo.

When I pulled up the drive, I didn't see Rollo's truck and wondered if it was in the garage. Parking, I hopped out and headed toward the garage. There was no one in there. Turning toward the house, I spotted the lights on in the barn and headed there instead.

Walking into the big open space I called out for Rollo and then for Zeke. There was no response. What the hell was going on? Turning around, I pulled out my cell and headed toward the house. I ran right into Dixie and she didn't make any attempt to apologize or to get out of my way.

Sighing, I tried being civil. "Hey. Have you seen Zeke or Rollo? Zeke texted me saying that Rollo was in trouble."

Smirking, she confirmed, "Oh, he's in trouble for sure."

Shaking my head, I spit out, "I don't have time for you games Dixie. Please tell me where he is."

"He's not here." I turned to see Zeke walk in the side door behind me and a majority of the pack followed in behind him. "We need to talk, Mina."

I grew panicked knowing I couldn't take them all on by myself. When I looked behind Dixie, the main barn door was blocked with pack members as well.

"We need to clear the air about a few things." Zeke closed the distance between us as I tried to remain calm. "Do you know why Rollo really came to Woodland Creek?" I just shook my head. "Well, it was for you, but not like you think."

What was he talking about?

"You were his mark." He paused. Stifling a laugh he added, "I can tell by your expression that you're confused. You were his mark, target, next project. He came here to kill you, just like he killed Scott, and just like he killed your mother."

There was no way. Anger flooded me as I lunged at him, but was quickly restrained by two large men. "You're a liar." I spit on him and he just wiped it away like it was nothing.

"Did he tell you how he got that shoulder injury?" I just stared at him, refusing to believe a word he said. "Your mother had a guest that night and he put up quite the fight. But nothing like our Rollo. Even as a teenager he was bigger and stronger than most men."

The tears threatened as he started describing my childhood home to me. Then he talked about how Rollo couldn't get himself to kill a kid and that was the only reason I was spared that night. I was going to be sick.

"Don't worry. He'll be here soon enough to confirm everything." Then he took his index finger and ran it across my jaw. "Until then we're going to have some fun." He jerked his head and the two goons dragged me to the center beam in the middle of the barn.

"Zeke. Let me go or you're going to regret this." I tried fighting against them, but I was no match for their strength.

"No, I don't think I will."

I had no other choice but to use my magic, but before I could focus, searing pain shot through the side of my head and everything went black.

When I came to, I was naked except for my shirt and panties. And the shirt was tattered. I was strung up by my wrists and couldn't feel my arms, the blood supply gone from them.

"Ah, the beauty awakes."

My blurry vision worked hard to focus. When everything became clear I noticed that I was the only woman in the room. This wasn't good. My body didn't feel like it had been violated in that way, but I had a feeling that's what was about to happen.

Zeke moved closer to me and with everything I had, I used my abdominal muscles and threw my legs up and out kicking him in the gut. He fell back, holding his torso, and coughing profusely. The moment I closed my eyes, everything went black again.

ROLLO

The commotion coming from the back of the property had me instantly on edge. Something was terribly wrong. All the trucks were here, including Mina's. When I walked into the barn, what I saw had me seeing red. Mina was tied by all fours, spread eagle, and barely able to stand. Her clothes were gone, only a tattered shirt and underwear donned her body, and she appeared to be unconscious. Someone was going to die for this.

"Mina!" I looked around, smelling everyone but not seeing anyone. Where had they gone? Bellowing out, "I know you're here. What's going on?" As I rushed to her, I pulled the knife I always carried from my pocket and began undoing her binds.

A small whimper escaped her lips and I was thankful to hear it. It meant she was alive. The temperatures were below freezing and I had no idea how long she'd been strung up there. After cutting both her legs free, I cradled her to my chest and swung her up into my arms.

"Mina, you need to wake up." I moved to a corner where I thought we'd be safe and set her down on a pile of blankets. Stroking her face, she became agitated as she tried scurrying away from me. "Mina, it's me."

When her eyes opened and registered upon my face, I saw two emotions. Relief and anger. "Get away from me!" She tried scrambling to her feet and fought off my attempts to help her.

"Mina, let me help you."

"Help me! This is *your* fault. How long were you planning to keep up the act?"

"What are you talking about?"

"Come on Rollo, tell her." I turned to the sound of Zeke's voice and saw the entire pack with him, including our mother. She wasn't supposed to be here for a few more days.

"This isn't happening. I already told you." I stepped toward Zeke making my challenge obvious. He was outwardly defying me and I'd had enough. What I didn't expect was for him to challenge me back. "Zeke, this is enough."

"Yes, we agree. This is enough. Enough of you doing your own thing. We think it's time for a new leader. One who follows through with orders and puts his people first." He motioned toward Mina, "Not some hussy."

"You want to talk about following through with orders? I'm the leader, I make the orders." Pointing at Victoria, I bellowed, "Your reign of terror ends NOW!" I stepped closer to Zeke and looked down upon the man I'd considered a brother my entire life. "Are we done here?"

"We filled Mina in on everything. She knows it all. Time to choose, Rollo."

I looked to Mina, who was visibly shaking, and refused to make eye contact with me. "Mina, whatever they told you, it's not true."

Zeke started laughing. "You stupid fuck. You're going to lose everything for a piece of ass."

I shoved him back and spit out, "Are you challenging me for pack leader?"

"Damn straight I am."

"You can fucking have it." Pointing behind me, "She's innocent and I will not have the blood of another innocent on my hands." Looking to my pack, "If you want Zeke as your leader, that's fine. For those who aren't with me, get the fuck off my property. You're trespassing."

I turned away from Zeke, not expecting the sucker punch in the back. Stumbling half a step forward, I stood tall before turning on him. My eyes caught a glimpse of Mina. I could tell that she was nervous and unsure of what to do and whom to believe.

"Mina, get out of here."

My mother stepped in front of her and proclaimed, "She's not going anywhere."

Before I could object, Zeke attacked me. Mina flinched before two of Zeke's cronies grabbed a hold of her. They were all going to pay for this. But first, I had to get Zeke to see sense. Our mother had been lying to us. I still wasn't entirely sure what about, but nothing added up anymore. Zeke was strong regardless of how much smaller than me he was. I shoved him back, not wanting to have this fight, but knowing it was the only thing that would stop this madness.

"You let her go right now!" Nobody even flinched. The wind was knocked from my chest as Zeke rammed me in the gut with his head, both of us falling back. "Zeke! This is madness. You're my brother."

"You were never *my* brother."

His words cut, but I didn't have time to think about it. Was he really prepared to fight to the death for something I told him he could have? If he wanted to lead the pack, so be it. I was long over it. The only thoughts in my mind were Mina and a future with her. We grappled and both got in a few good hits. When I gained the advantage and we both stood, legs wavering, and chests heaving, he put up his hands in what I thought was surrender.

Before I knew it there were four men on me as the two who held Mina brought her forward. Looking to

Mina, her eyes flashed that white-blue, and I knew what she had in mind. Though, I was going to try to get us out of there before going to those extremes. She had gained remarkable control over her powers in the passing weeks and we had the advantage since the pack didn't fully know about her abilities. I shook my head at her, hoping she knew that I wanted her to wait.

The woman I'd always considered my mother stepped forward holding a large carving knife. "Tonight is the blood moon. We'll make our sacrifice and the Spitz line will finally be stricken from this world. The Frost line, unworthy to rule, will also be vanquished. Zeke, my son. Come here."

What the fuck was happening? There was no time to find out. I looked to Mina and nodded. She closed her eyes, so that no one would suspect, and the thunder came. It wasn't long before the barn doors blew open garnering everyone's attention. The sky had grown dark as rain pelted the exterior of the wood walls.

As the barn walls began to shake, the pack grew nervous. The grip on me was loosened and I took advantage of it. Freeing myself, I stalked toward Mina and the two men holding her released her reluctantly, as my mother screamed her objections. With Mina safely at my side, I pointed my finger at my mother and cursed her.

"I'm not finished with you."

She slashed out at me with her knife which I grabbed. As it sliced into my hand I held it firm and grabbed her wrist with my other hand, snapping her forearm in half. Her shrills filled the space and when I released her, she fell to the ground. Keeping my hand clenched as the warmth of the blood seeped over my fingers, Mina and I took off.

When we reached my truck, the storm dying down, she climbed in the passenger side and me behind the driver's seat. We took off, though my bloody hand was slipping on the wheel.

"Rollo!"

I swerved, nearly missing a tree. "Take the wheel."

She did as I ordered as I tore off a piece of my shirt and wrapped it around my hand as best I could. Once that was done I took the wheel back and reached my other hand out to her. She flinched and practically crawled into the passenger door.

"Don't touch me."

"Mina?"

"Zeke told me everything." She glared at me. "You came to Woodland Creek to kill me. Why not just get it over with?"

"Please, let me explain."

"Explain what? That you fucking played me? Pursued me until I gave in like a fool? I knew I shouldn't have trusted you."

I pulled down a dirt road and when I was certain we weren't being followed, I pulled off the road and threw the truck into park. "Listen to me right now. Yes, I came here to Woodland Creek and you were my target." She stared blank faced back at me. "Nothing added up and I started doing my own reconnaissance to try to find the truth. A letter from Scott, or Jude, also grew my suspicions. What I didn't expect was to fall in love with you, Mina."

"NO! Don't you dare." The tears were falling from her eyes as she wiped at them aggressively. "This whole thing has been a sham. I'm such an idiot." She pulled her knees up and buried her face in her hands, my fingers still itching to touch her.

"Mina, please forgive me. I should've told you, but I knew you had secrets of your own and I didn't want to scare you away."

"Well you did a pretty damn good job." I stared at her as her swollen eyes met mine. "Not only did I trust you, I fell for you. You've destroyed that, destroyed me."

I tried reaching for her again as she scrambled out the door. "MINA!"

Jumping out after her, I watched her shift and then take off. Scrubbing my hands over my face, I winced at the wound. Did I follow her or give her space? I didn't know what the fuck to do, but I knew I couldn't run on my injured hand.

"Rollo?"

Startled, I turned to see Jack. He was alone and I eyed him suspiciously. His family had deep ties to Zeke's, but he had a good heart. "Jack?"

"What they're doing isn't right. I'm with you.

What can I do to prove it?"

"Start talking."

Jack spilled everything. Zeke's plan all along had been to claim pack leader and if it meant killing me, he was prepared to do so. Mina was also a mission he planned to complete since I hadn't. He shared the same obsession as his mother that Mina needed to die.

The only thing Jack wasn't privy to was why. Why did Zeke and Victoria have this fixation on Mina? What secret was still hidden that we had yet to uncover? Something in Mina's past had to be linked to something Victoria didn't want anyone to know about. But what was it?

I needed to find Mina. She wasn't safe and I had to convince her that she needn't fear me. I was the one trying to protect her. We also needed to go see Jillian again. She had mentioned a spell that could take Mina back to the night of her mother's murder, but Mina had refused. I couldn't blame her. But it may be the key to uncovering what none of us knew. Who killed Mora and why?

MINA

It hurt to breathe. My heart was broken and I didn't know how to fix it. I had to keep myself under control. I didn't want to hurt any innocent people, but I also wanted to lose myself in my powers. What Zeke had told me was true. Rollo came to Woodland Creek to kill me. I had a target on my back and had no idea why.

Sitting down in the grass, I clasped my hands on the back of my head. What was I missing? Victoria wouldn't elude to why she wanted me dead, just that it needed to happen. I couldn't go back to my place, that'd be the first place they'd look for me. The shop was out, too. There was only one place I could turn.

Shifting back, I ran off through the woods. I sat on the property line for a while, observing until I thought for sure I was safe. I made my way to the back door and pawed at the wood door. I could hear the cats inside going crazy and then a few lights turned on.

Amy pulled the curtain aside and jumped when I barked. Her eyes found me and then she opened the door.

"Mina? What are you doing here?"

I looked around and whimpered. Not wanting to shift, but I had no choice. I stood, trying to cover myself as she blushed.

"I'm sorry. Here." She removed the long cardigan she wore and wrapped it around me. "Come in. Are you ok?" I started sobbing and she had me follow her upstairs.

Sitting on her bed, she pulled some clothes out of her dresser and handed them to me. She showed me to the bathroom and drew a bath for me. I hadn't had a bath in ages and couldn't wait to sink under the water. Amy tended to me like a sister or a mother would and scrubbed my back and then my hair. Thoughts of my mother bombarded me and I started crying all over again.

"Mina, I'm so sorry. Is there anything I can do to help?" Amy was sincere and I was grateful.

Shaking my head and wiping at my nose, I shakily said, "I think I want Jillian to do the spell. I need to know what happened to my mother. I was there, but I can't remember. I think it's the only thing that is going to stop all this madness."

"Ok. We'll tell her in the morning. You should get some rest." Draining the water, I stood as she wrapped a towel around me. "You can stay in my room. I'll be right next door if you need anything."

She motioned at another door in the bathroom, pointing out that the rooms were adjoined through the bathroom. "Ok. I can stay there. I don't want to take your room."

"Nope, I insist."

I managed to get myself dressed and crawled under the covers after she combed out my hair. The attention was soothing and had me completely relaxed. I was vaguely aware of the lights going out and Amy wishing me a good night's rest. My heart still ached for Rollo, but I couldn't release any more tears. I knew we needed to talk, but I knew my body would betray me if I let him get too close.

I woke in the morning to a knock on my door and Amy asking to come in. Waving her in, I looked to the clock to discover I'd slept most of the morning away. Then it dawned on me that I had clients today.

"Shit. I have to get to the shop."

"It's taken care of. I posted a note that you had an emergency to tend to. And with everything going on, it's not safe for you to be there anyway."

How did she know? I hadn't told her anything last night, except that Rollo and I were over. "What are you talking about?"

"He's here. Has been all night. Slept outside on the porch." She giggled, "It's really quite endearing. He loves you, Mina. Are you sure you can't work it out?"

With my eyes downcast, my throat tightened as I confessed. "I love him, too, but it's complicated. You don't know everything."

She sat down next to me and took my hand. "I think I do. He explained everything to Grams and I this morning."

My head jerked up as I questioned her, "Everything?"

"He was sent here to kill you, but instead he fell for you. So he started doing research of his own to try to figure out why his stepmother wanted you dead." She took a deep breath and smiled at me as I closed my jaw. "Is that everything?"

"Yeah, I guess. If he's being truthful."

"Listen, you're a Thomas by blood. You're safe in this house and nothing can hurt you. Get dressed and come eat. We're in the kitchen. Grams is a good judge of character. If she didn't trust him, he wouldn't still be here."

She left the room, my cousin. I don't know why it just then resonated with me that she *was* family. She was my cousin. She was odd and peculiar, but I'm sure they thought the same thing about me. I spotted some clothes at the end of the bed that weren't there last night. Magic or had she come in earlier to find me still asleep? It didn't matter. It was time to be a big girl and face my big bad wolf. I smiled at that and knew already my body was betraying me where Rollo was concerned.

Making my way downstairs, the smell of food overtook my senses as my stomach grumbled. Almost anything I could ever want for breakfast was laid out on the kitchen counter. I took a little bit of everything, loading my plate. I sat down at the small table in the corner and began eating. The thump of his boots on the hardwood floor immediately got my attention.

Keeping my eyes on my food, I listened as he moved around the room. He was pouring a glass of something and within moments a glass of orange juice was placed in front of me. The metal legs of the chair across from me scraped along the floor and then he sat down. I spotted his bandaged hand resting on the table as his fingers lightly drummed on the tabletop.

"Is this your plan, to ignore me?"

I didn't say anything, just kept eating.

"Mina, stop acting like a child and talk to me." I looked up at him and with a smug look shoved more bacon in my mouth and smiled sardonically at him. "Don't choke."

Rolling my eyes, I removed them from his face and gazed back at my plate. We sat in silence and soon I couldn't eat anymore. Pushing the plate away, he immediately took it to the sink and cleared the few remaining contents. I slithered out of my chair and attempted to head out of the kitchen.

His hand came down on my bare wrist, his touch scalding me. Warmth spread through my entire body as my fingers curled into themselves, my nails digging into the palm of my hand. All my strength gave way as he came closer to me. His other hand ran over the back of my head and through my hair the way he always did. I had to close my eyes to try to hide the emotion in my eyes.

Letting him pull me to his chest, I inhaled deeply as he started apologizing. "Mina, please don't shut me out. I'm so sorry. I promise you since the first moment I laid eyes on you, all thoughts of why I came to Woodland Creek left me. I'll die before I let anything happen to you. Please say you believe me."

I knew what I was going to say before I said it and I hated myself for it. "I believe you, but I'm still hurt." His arms wrapped tighter around me as I gently held onto the material of his shirt.

"Please look at me, Sweetheart." His hands cupped my face as I tilted my head up to his, refusing to open my eyes. His nose ran along mine. "Please let me see them." I let them flutter open and instantly lost myself in his green-blue depths. "I love those eyes and everything behind them." He kissed me softly as my eyes flickered shut.

Whimpering, I pulled away before it got too heated. "Please, Rollo. Take it slow, I'm still trying to wrap my mind around everything."

Smiling, he kissed my nose. "Of course."

Jillian walked into the room then. "Alright. Since you two finally have everything figured out, it's time to get down to business." My Grandma, though it was still strange referring to her that way, was blunt to a fault and it made her very endearing.

Sitting down in the living room, the four of us began discussing what would come next. I agreed to take the potion. If it worked the way it was supposed to, I'd be taken back to my childhood and I'd be able to retell what had happened all those years ago. I shot back the liquid and began coughing at its horrid taste.

Latching onto Rollo's hand, I felt the room begin to spin and I couldn't keep my eyes open any longer.

"Mina, are you there?" I was aware of Grandma Jillian talking to me, but I couldn't quite get my mouth to work.

~ YOUNG MINA ~

"Mina, are you there, sweetie?"

"Yes, mom!" I yelled from the spot on my bed as I flipped through the pages of my book.

"Please come down, Mina. Your Uncle Scott will be here any moment."

Huffing, I climbed off my bed and headed to the kitchen. Mom was headed out with that Jude guy again. It wasn't that I disliked him, but I preferred Uncle Scott. He was watching me tonight while Mom went out and I was looking forward to it. He always let me stay up late and was teaching me how to play poker, though my mom didn't know.

I heard his truck pull in the drive and ran out to greet him. Jumping on his back, he carried me back into the house and dropped me on the couch.

"I need to talk to your mom, kiddo. Give us a minute okay?"

"Sure thing." I went back to my room and didn't think anything of it until I heard their voices getting loud.

"Scott, I'm not discussing this with you. I know what he's done, but he's trying. I love him. Can't you understand that?"

"Yes, because I love *you*. He's never taken care of the two of you the way he should."

My mom's voice grew sad and I didn't quite understand what they were talking about. Who'd never taken care of us? My father? Uncle Scott always told me he didn't know who my father was. The front door opened and I saw Jude come in. He'd overheard the same conversation and smiled at me. Embarrassed that he'd caught me, I slammed my door shut.

A few minutes later the front door closed again and I heard a car, Jude's car, pull away. A knock came to my door and Uncle Scott poked his head inside.

"You heard that didn't ya?" I nodded. "I'm sorry kiddo."

"Uncle Scott, do you know who my daddy is?"

Sighing, "I do, but I promised your mom I'd let her tell you. She's going to tell you soon."

I started crying, "I want you to be my daddy."

He wrapped an arm around me and said, "I want that, too. But, I'll always be your Uncle and uncles are way cooler. I get to let you stay up late, eat junk food, and teach you how to play Poker. Dads have to be responsible." I laughed at that and agreed. "Now. How about we go get some pizza? And if you're good, we'll stop for ice cream on the way home."

"Yes!"

I went to bed with a belly ache, but fell asleep almost immediately. Scott would probably fall asleep on the couch like he often did. That meant I'd get his yummy French toast in the morning.

When I woke, it was the middle of the night and there was some shouting coming from the living room. I was used to this kind of thing happening. Before Jude,

Mom had some boyfriends who liked to break things. Jude was probably the same way. Then sounds I wasn't familiar with began to fill my ears.

Not knowing what to do, I hid under my bed until everything went silent. My door opened and I had to cover my mouth to keep quiet. A pair of old brown work boots circled my bed and then left the room. It seems I waited forever to come out. Everything was quiet for a long time before I decided to leave my room and see if everything was ok. When I walked through the living room, the room was destroyed. Broken glass and toppled furniture was all I could see. And blood. There was blood on the floor and walls.

Everything went silent and then a ringing in my ears began. Walking to the kitchen, I saw my mother's lifeless body, covered in red, on the floor. On the other side of the room was Uncle Scott. He was sitting up against the lower cabinets, not moving, eyes open, and was also covered in blood.

The back door opened and a panic-stricken Jude walked in. He took in the scene and locked eyes with me. Moving his hands in front of my face, he chanted,

"You will forget you saw this, Mina. All you will remember is that your mother was murdered and Jude disappeared."

My eyes grew heavy as I fell into Jude's arms. I think I fell asleep because I was startled awake when my bedroom door opened later. I had no recollection of what had happened.

"Mina? Oh, God. Please, no. MINA!"

Recognizing Scott's voice, I sat up and climbed out of bed. "I'm here."

Pulling me to his chest, he was sobbing. "Thank, God. My girl. I thought you were gone." He examined my face and arms, asking, "You're not hurt?" I just shook my head. Something was different about him, but I couldn't quite place it. "Come on. We need to go."

"Go? Where?"

"You're staying at my place tonight, ok?"

"What about Mom?"

He closed his eyes for a long time before saying, "We'll talk about it tomorrow. Let's get you home and to bed."

I didn't argue. I was familiar with Scott's house, though he seemed to forget that because he almost put me in the wrong bedroom. I had my own designated bedroom at Scott's which made me feel very special.

The next few months were incredibly hard. The doctors said I'd forgotten any details due to the trauma. My mother was dead and Jude was gone. Scott never left my side and took guardianship of me since my mother didn't have any other family. My mother's shop ended up getting boarded up, but Scott promised that one day we'd get it back. I didn't believe him, no longer caring about anything. The only thing I cared about was getting my revenge.

ROLLO

Mina was recounting her story to Jillian and even her voice sounded young again. This odd sense of dread washed over me as I pulled Amy out of the room.

"When did this happen?" She looked at me strangely. "I can't recall the date. Do you remember?" Nodding, she shuffled through a stack of newspapers and handed it to me.

Finding the date and then reading the story over and over again, I sank into a chair as horror filled me. It was around the same time I'd injured my troublesome shoulder. Several of my father's men were headed out on a mission, but I hadn't been told where or what, and since I'd injured myself I couldn't go. It was shortly after my father had died and Victoria was leading the pack.

Was it just coincidence or was my family responsible for this? I caught what Mina said, that Scott had been dead. But if that was the case, how had he been the one to come back and retrieve her later on? Was he just caught in the crossfire or was he an intended target, too? I can't imagine if he was an intended target that Victoria would let him live after finding out he was alive.

Jillian was pulling Mina from her trance and helped lay her down on the couch. "She needs to sleep for a while. We should talk." Covering Mina with a blanket, I then followed Jillian and Amy into the kitchen.

"I'm confused."

"You caught that? Yes. I have a feeling I know what happened." I narrowed my eyes at her. "Just hear me out."

Nodding, I encouraged her to speak. "I'm listening."

"Remember when I said Jude liked to play tricks on people?" I nodded. "He was a master of disguise and could take on the appearance of almost anyone for short periods of time."

Confused, I asked, "Like a shifter?"

"Kind of, but where you only take one form, he could take any. Now, if he cast a spell with the blood of his intended target, there's a good chance he could make it permanent."

I shook my head and pressed my eyes shut. "So, you're saying you think Jude took on the appearance of Scott?" She nodded. "This is insane and that still doesn't answer the question about who killed Scott and Mora. And why did they leave Mina unharmed?"

173

"I know how crazy it sounds. But if Jude knew, and I suspect he did, that Mina was his child, he'd do anything and everything to protect her, even if that meant becoming someone else. Based on what Mina just told us, Jude was probably aware of her bond with Scott so he used it to his advantage."

What didn't make sense to me was that if it was my family behind Mora's murder, then they likely killed Scott, too. Why had they never come after him again? Then it dawned on me. Maybe they'd been successful in killing Mora and Scott found her, and being distraught took his own life. Or, what if Jude had walked in and assumed Scott had killed Mora and in turn killed Scott? My head was spinning from the possibilities.

"What is it boy? Something's troubling you."

There was no point in hiding it. "My stepmother is obsessed with Mina and killing her and I believe she's behind Mora's death. But that doesn't explain the rest of it."

She agreed and said, "We have some more digging to do. There's no telling what other magic Jude placed on Mina to suppress any other memories through the years."

"Will she remember what she told us today?"

"Yes. She's going to be upset. Especially if she figures out the possibility that Scott has been dead this whole time and that Jude was the one raising her all along; her father."

"Christ. I can't take this. This will undo her."

"She's survived worse. She'll get through it. But you need to decide if you're going to be there with her, because if you're not... You should leave now."

"No, I'm not abandoning her."

"That's what I thought." She patted my cheek and added, "I also think we should exhume Scott's body...Jude's body. That will help give us more answers." Then she left the room.

I didn't want to think about what we might find, but an empty coffin was one thought. More things started to confuse me. If Scott was really Jude, why hadn't he left everything to Mina? It made no sense. He had no loyalty to me. Did he know or suspect that Victoria was behind everything? And writing that letter to me. How did he know I'd pay any heed to it? I had to stop thinking about it before I drove myself mad. I also had to come to the realization that we may never know.

When Mina woke and recounted what she'd told us, she was nearly inconsolable. Especially when she asked why she thought Scott was dead if he wasn't. Then she put the pieces together and wondered what we all did. Was Scott really Jude, or Jude Scott? Through it all she managed to hold her temper, or the powers that came with her temper.

Later that day I started the paperwork to have Scott's body exhumed. Thank God for my powers of persuasion at the police station. It worked like a charm, but it would take some time. The ground was already getting hard and there was a chance we'd have to wait until Spring since it was already November.

Mina and I kept low profiles and stayed at the Thomas house. The next night, we lay in bed talking. She made it clear that I wouldn't be getting lucky.

"Mina, just let me hold you." She curled into my side and I could feel the tension roll off of her as she began to relax. "I've been thinking. Your ties to Woodland Creek seem pretty strong. Would your fellow shifters stand by your side against Zeke if it came down to that?"

She didn't move and I could sense that she was thinking about it. "Most probably would. Some are very reclusive and don't want to get involved, but Debi..."

"Debi's a shifter?"

She laughed softly, "Yes. You didn't know?"

"I guess I never really took notice."

"Well, Debi and most of the regulars at Vider's are all shifters and they would gladly form a united front for one of their own." She took a deep breath. "You really don't think they'll just leave it be, do you?"

"I'm afraid I don't. Zeke holds a grudge, learned it from his mother."

Her voice became heated. "There's no fucking grudge to hold. I didn't do anything and if something happened between Victoria and my mother... Well, Victoria needs to get over it. My mother is dead and nothing is going to change that."

"I understand, truly I do. Tomorrow, why don't you see if we can get all your people together? I can check in with Jack and see if there's any new info. We can go from there and see what we're dealing with." She nodded and relaxed again in my arms. "I just want you safe. You're my top concern." She didn't respond, but I didn't expect her to.

Several moments later she asked quietly, "Do you ever just want to get up and leave? Woodland Creek is my home, but it's all I've ever known and I want more than that."

Exhaling, I confided in her, "That's how I felt about where I was before. I have, or had, a pack. Almost everything I could ever want or need, but they're not my home. I don't want any of the titles or bullshit that comes with the territory. I just want a family and a life of my own."

"All I've ever wanted was a pack to call home and all you want is a home with no pack. We're a match made in hell."

"I don't need a home or a pack if I have you." She tilted her chin up and looked at me. "I mean it, Mina.

You're the only thing I want."

"I want that, too. But let's get through the next few days before we go making promises we're not prepared to keep."

"I'm prepared to keep all my promises, Mina. Are you?"

"Rollo, please."

I could hear the strain in her voice and I wasn't trying to pressure her. I was just more willing to proclaim what I wanted. She wasn't there yet. "I'm sorry. You're right. We need to get some rest."

The next morning I crawled out of bed, leaving her to sleep. I went for a run and then called Jack. He said he'd meet me and that he had some info for me. About an hour later he pulled up in his car and climbed into the passenger seat of my truck.

"They're not planning on leaving any time soon. They've taken over your house and they're going through everything. I don't know what they're looking for, but it's something."

I slammed my hand down on the steering wheel. "What the hell are they looking for? I've got to be missing something obvious, but what?"

Before I could pull away, my vehicle was surrounded by cars and trucks. Zeke, Dixie, and Victoria stepped out of the truck behind us and headed my way. I'd already pulled my knife on Jack who swore it wasn't a setup.

"I told you to make sure you weren't followed."

"I did, I swear."

Zeke chimed in, "It's called a tracker, Rollo."

Holding the knife to Jack's throat, I grossly miscalculated Zeke's harshness. "I know he's your cousin, Zeke, but you come any closer and I'll slit his throat."

Zeke turned to the others, shrugged his shoulders and pulled out a gun. Aiming it at Jack, he shot him square in the chest and then laughed. "Never did care for narcs."

Wiping the blood spray from my face, I wiped my hand on my jeans. "Jesus Christ, Zeke. What is wrong with you?"

I knew that one of us was going to end up dead, if not both of us, by the time this was over. What I didn't expect was for the tranquilizer gun that Dixie pulled out and used on me. Yanking the dart out of my arm, I tried fighting off its immediate dose of drowsiness, but it was pointless.

When I woke, I was in the barn, strung up the same way that Mina had been. Yanking on my binds, there was no way I'd be escaping. Mina was out there unprotected. I tried guessing the time based on the amount of daylight left hanging in the sky, but couldn't be certain. My best guess was that it was early evening.

"He's awake." Zeke walked over and the rest of the pack followed in behind him, including Victoria and her casted arm. "Now, tell us where she is and we'll go easy on you."

"Fuck you. I'm not telling you anything."

Victoria pulled out that same carving knife and my hand immediately ached in response. Jillian and Amy had cleaned it and bandaged it, but it was still a fresh wound.

"I'm guessing I can get you to speak." She began cutting the clothes from my body until the only thing that remained were my pants. She grabbed hold of my dick and I cringed in disgust. Leaning into my ear she disgusted me with her words. "You're much larger than your father. It's a shame I didn't know that sooner."

She then stepped back and slowly ran the blade down my chest. I refused to cry out and controlled my breathing as best I could. Soon I felt the warmth of the blood trickling through my chest hair.

"Ready to talk yet?"

MINA

I woke to find Rollo gone. According to Jillian and Amy, he'd gone to meet Jack and wanted me to start calling people to get our plan in motion. After showering and getting dressed, I did just that. I called Debi first and she agreed and began calling everyone she could think of while I called some of the shop owners in town that I hoped would help.

A few hours later I was still waiting on Rollo. He wasn't answering his phone and no one had heard or seen him. Dread was beginning to fill me. That was about the time Debi showed up and had several people with her. When I stepped into the yard to greet her, she immediately knew something was wrong.

Rushing over to me, she wrapped her arms around

me, "What is it, Mina?"

"He's not answering his phone. He should be back by now." My voice was cracking and I knew this was a side of me that Debi wasn't used to.

"Calm down sweetie. Let's go inside and try calling him again. Ok?"

Once we were inside, with shaky hands I dialed Rollo's phone again. This time someone answered, but it wasn't Rollo.

"Mina! Just the person we've been looking for."

I was going to be sick. "Where is he, Zeke?"

"Around. Well, pieces of him anyway." What the hell did that mean? "How about we barter? You come here and we'll let your friends live."

He was full of shit and we all knew I was going to go there with or without any bargain. "Hope you're ready for rain." I disconnected the call and threw the phone to the ground, uncaring if I'd broken it.

"What's going on?"

I filled Debi, Jillian, and Amy in on what Zeke had said. The others had remained outside, not comfortable heading into the home of wizards.

Stepping outside, we filled in the others and devised our plan.

Woodland Creek was our town and we'd be damned if Zeke and his crew were going to try to run us out of our own home. In our ranks we had a few bears, panthers, leopards, a gargoyle, deadly snakes and spiders and many more. Then with my power and Jillian's, there wasn't any reason we couldn't overpower Zeke and his minions. The question was if we were too late to save Rollo.

We loaded up in our vehicles, *Hurricane* by Thirty Seconds To Mars playing in Debi's car. I tried to remain calm as we took the dirt roads. The property was almost entirely dark as we approached. Most of us parked down the road and walked the rest of the way. I knew the property better than most, but it'd been a long time since I ran the acreage. We knew that they had to be waiting for us, but there was no other option. We made it to the back of the property and there appeared to be one solitary light on in the barn.

Debi and her sister flanked me as we cautiously opened the barn door. It was quiet and all I could smell was blood and Rollo. I forced myself to keep calm as I scanned my flashlight through the dark space.

"Over there." Debi elbowed me and I followed the direction of her finger.

Rollo was hanging from almost the exact same spot I had been just a couple days prior. As I got closer to him, the stench of blood was turning my stomach. He had several cuts on his chest, some worse than others. His face was also bloodied and they'd cut his hair. The long ponytail lay in the straw at his feet.

Reaching out to him, I stroked his cheek and whispered his name, "Rollo..." He was warm and I could breathe. "Help me get him down."

Just as we finished cutting him free, the three of us barely able to support his weight, the barn doors flung open and the lights turned on. Setting Rollo on the floor as gently as I could, Debi, Diane, and I formed a circle around him. Zeke, Dixie, Victoria, and every other traitor walked in. Having heard no commotion I had to hope and assume that the rest of my party was simply biding their time.

"I owe you an ass-whooping, bitch." Dixie's

comment surprised me.

"Really. You want to do this now?" I'd easily taken her when she'd launched her surprise attack on me all those weeks ago. "You want me to kick your ass again...fine by me."

She took another step forward and Zeke put his arm out to stop her as Victoria proclaimed, "We don't have time for this. Let's get this over with."

"Can I just ask you one question?" Victoria sneered at me for a moment before nodding. "Why did you kill my mother?"

Pursing her lips, she then answered, "Figured that out did you?"

"What could my mother have ever done to you?"

"Your bitch of a mother tried taking what was mine. After Rollo's mother died—an unfortunate accident—his father needed a new bride. All fingers pointed at Mora since she was the last surviving member of one of the founding families. If she was gone, I was the choice."

"Seriously. This is all over a guy? You're crazier than you look."

Victoria took another step closer. "Your mother agreed, but her heart was elsewhere, with Scott, or so I assumed. Turned out Scott was trying to help her come up with a plan to leave town before the wedding. She was in love, just not with Scott. When I overheard her telling Scott she was pregnant, I seized my opportunity and had her banished. I assumed Scott was your father, but when she was confronted she said it was someone else."

My mother was in love with Jude? If that was the case, why had it taken so long for them to come forward with the truth? I didn't have time to think about it and didn't even know if what I was being told was the truth.

"Ok, but that doesn't explain why you want *me* dead."

"You're the last surviving Spitz."

Power. It was all about power. "You think I want your make believe crown? I don't. You can leave and I promise you neither Rollo nor I will ever challenge you."

"Sorry. It doesn't work that way. The Spitz line contains powers and I plan to have those transferred to me."

"What bullshit powers? We have a specialty for healing. That's it."

"So your grandmother hasn't told you everything has she? It's not just the Spitz power in you, but the Thomas power and if combined with my power, well. That's what I want and I'm going to get it."

I was struggling to keep up with her brand of crazy. She could have my fucking weather related powers and choke on them. Just as I was ready to speak, I sensed movement behind me and found Rollo attempting to get to his feet. Immediately, I tried to help support him.

"Victoria, this is enough. Zeke, don't you see she's crazy?"

"Her interests have always been for my betterment."

"How many mothers are you going to let her kill before you wake up? Hell, she probably killed your own father for your *betterment*!"

The barn doors opened once again, Woodland Creek shifters making their presence known. Jillian wasn't with them and I prayed she was safe somewhere while watching over us. If things got bad, her powers and mine were the two things we were all counting on.

Zeke came forward and challenged Rollo. "How about we finish this, here and now?"

My eyes got big as I watched Rollo step toward him. He was in no condition to fight. Trying to step in front of him, I pleaded with him, "Rollo you're hurt. You can't do this."

"Aww, ain't she sweet? Come on Rollo, unless you want your bitch to fight for you."

The growl that left Rollo's throat had me even more worried for him. He needed to be smart, not caught up in anger for this fight. Zeke had already proven that he was willing to fight dirty. "Rollo?"

Pushing me off of him, he stepped closer to Zeke. "Man to man or dog to dog?"

Debi pulled me back to her side, Diane on the other side of me. I was worried that this was just a ploy, a distraction. Victoria and Zeke weren't just going to let me, or anyone, walk out of here tonight. Zeke removed his shirt and they faced each other like men, both topless, as they began circling one another. Zeke was bouncing back and forth from one foot to the other as Rollo just watched, calculating Zeke's movement.

Zeke took the first swing and Rollo took the hit to the ribs with great ease. My eyes closed. I never did like boxing or fighting of any kind, even though I'd been in my share of fights growing up.

Turning my head, I kept my eyes on the rest of the room. Whispering in Debi's ear, I said, "Tell me when it's over or if I need to get involved." She simply nodded and that's when I noticed that Dixie was missing. Shit!

ROLLO

There was no way Mina was going to fight this battle for me. This ended tonight. We fought and grappled and I struggled. My injuries were worse than I wanted to admit, but there was no way I was going to stand down. I needed to focus.

I managed to take him by surprise and swept his legs out from under him. When he landed on his back, I let him be. I needed every spare second to catch my bearings. And I knew from a lifetime of fighting beside him, that if he got angry he would make mistakes.

And that's just what he did. He jumped up and hurled himself at me, but I was ready for him. I busted his nose and the sound of it filled the barn. Gasps and groans were exchanged as blood poured from his nose. Part of me wanted him to beg for mercy, but I knew that was very unlikely. It was then that all hell broke loose. A gunshot rang through the air, but I couldn't tell where it came from.

Screaming began from behind me. Debi and Mina were huddled over the body of another woman. Debi began sobbing and I knew whoever it was that had been shot was important to her and therefore important to Mina.

Before I could even try to get a grip on matters, everyone began shifting and a war broke out. Zeke pounced on me in his husky form so I had no choice but to shift as well. My arm in his mouth, I quickly rolled him gaining the advantage. I was well aware of the thunder and lightning that started overhead.

I tried finding her in the mob, but couldn't. Zeke growled behind me and I turned to prepare for his attack. Grabbing hold of his neck, I had him in the death grip. His whimpers were the only thing I could hear as his blood filled my mouth. Releasing him, he didn't move and he refused to make eye contact with me. It was over, or so I thought.

In the distance I could hear tornado sirens going off. Mina had outdone herself. I had to find her. Remaining in my husky form, I let my sense of smell find her. The progress she'd made was becoming well evident. I ran past more than a few pack members, loyal to Zeke, who were no longer breathing. It was a shame and all for nothing.

I found her in the field behind the barn. Victoria was creeping up behind her and I didn't think I'd make it there in time. Shifting back to human form I screamed for her, but she couldn't hear me over the howling of the wind. Just before Victoria struck her,

Jillian appeared and Victoria was thrown back by the simple movement of Jillian's hand.

Naked as a jaybird, I continued making my way toward Mina. Eyes aglow, she turned them on me. Another thing she'd accomplished, being able to focus through the power. The fighting was beginning to die down. Jillian and Victoria were in a standoff and Jillian didn't hesitate to make the fatal blow. Victoria crumbled to the ground and I prayed that vile bitch was dead.

Once everyone saw that Victoria was down, the fighting slowly ceased. All eyes seemed to be on Mina, everyone looking on in awe as she wielded her power. The winds died down and I went in search of Zeke, and clothes. My truck was the closest thing and I opened the door and pulled out a pair of sweats and yanked them on.

Another gunshot rang through the air and fear gripped me. Mina! As I ran back to where she was, I heard my name.

"ROLLO!" It was Zeke.

He stood in the field where Mina had been, but I

couldn't spot her. Then I saw her figure on the ground in the tall grass. No! Running toward her, I saw her begin to move.

"I'd stop if I were you, Rollo."

Slowing my pace, I looked to Zeke who had blood dripping down his neck from my bite marks. "Zeke, it's over. You won't make it out of here alive."

"If I'm dead, you're coming with me." He cocked the shot gun as the winds picked up again. "Dixie, NOW!"

Jerking my head back toward Mina, she was focused on me. She spotted Dixie in her shifter form, ready to pounce on her, but did nothing. We both made the ultimate sacrifice. I stepped between her and Zeke hoping she'd take the defense with Dixie. She didn't. A board from the barn flew overhead and nailed Zeke in the head causing him to drop the gun. I wasted no time and snapped his neck.

When I turned to Mina, it was in time to see her waver from all the power she'd consumed and Dixie attacked. Mina didn't stand a chance. My worst nightmare played out in front of me. Mina was limp on the ground and Dixie tossed her about like a ragdoll. When I reached them, I kicked Dixie in the gut and she flew off of Mina and then ran off.

Kneeling next to her, I cried out for Jillian. Mina was bleeding profusely from the neck and I didn't know how to stop it. Scooping her to my chest, foreign sobs ripped through my throat. I hadn't cried like this since my mother died when I was a young boy.

"Please Mina, don't leave me. I just found you." With shaky hands, I traced her face when Jillian knelt down next to us.

"Lay her down, son." Jillian began slowly waving her hands over her. "I can try to save her, but I don't know that I can save her powers."

I just shook my head. "I don't care about her powers just fix her."

"She may not be able to shift either. You know her better than I do. Will she be ok with that?"

Debi joined us and added, "Shifter doesn't define her. She'll get over it."

I nodded my agreement, but all I heard in my head was Mina talking about always wanting a pack of her own. It was idiotic to think that way. She was young and had so much ahead of her, shifter or not.

Jillian closed her eyes and began chanting. All the shifters gathered around Mina, some holding hands as we all said our silent prayers. Just when I thought all hope was lost, Mina took in a big breath and let it out just as quick. The color began to fill her face again, but she didn't open her eyes.

"I've done everything I can. The rest is up to her."

With some help, I placed her in the back of my truck. Jillian sat with her as I drove to the hospital. Debi followed behind with her sister Diane who was barely clinging to life, thanks also to Jillian. *Seven Devils* by Florence and The Machine was playing. The song had almost come to fruition. But we'd conquered our devils, I just prayed Mina lived to tell the story.

We told the ER staff that she'd been attacked by a stray dog and they believed it given her wounds. They gave her a transfusion and said that the hope was for her to regain consciousness soon.

We waited for over two days. During that time, Diane passed away and every last ounce of Debi's hope resided with Mina surviving. Chief of Police, TJ Rickman was circling like a hawk. I was beginning to think it was more out of concern for Mina and not out of suspicion to the few shifters now missing and the bodies of my pack that had been found in the woods.

If I was a suspect, he was keeping hush about it. But I had my alibi; Jillian, who also confirmed she was with Mina and me. I wasn't sure what had become of Victoria's body, but Jillian had assured me that it was taken care of. That old witch probably had over a dozen bodies buried in her yard, God love her.

I was sleeping in the corner chair when something woke me. Startled, my eyes tried focusing in the dimly lit room. She was stirring. I jumped up and rushed to her bedside. Stroking her face, I kissed her forehead and waited for her eyes to find me.

"Rollo?" Her voice was hoarse as she tried speaking. "What happened?"

"Shh, you're safe. Everything's ok. You're going to be ok."

Tears fell from her eyes. I wasn't able to console her long before her nurse came in and then the doctors. They ran their tests and brought her some liquids to drink. I smiled watching her down the three juice cartons they brought her.

"Take it easy, Mina. You're going to upset your stomach." The nurse warned her and then left the room.

She yawned and I urged her to go back to sleep. Shaking her head she asked, "Will you hold me? It's freezing in here."

That statement resonated with me. She was never cold. Maybe what Jillian was concerned about had happened. Was it possible her powers were gone or was it just the circumstances and the cold hospital room? I walked to the thermostat and increased the temperature before sitting on the bed next to her. Curling into my side, I think she was asleep before I could even get comfortable.

MINA

I'd been home for almost a week and was finally starting to feel like a human again. I was so weak and felt like I was sleeping my life away. The doctors assured me it was normal and to get my rest. Jillian was coming over that night to check on me and I was looking forward to seeing her.

The four of us sat down to eat; Rollo at my side and Jillian and Amy sat across from us. The carryout smelled delicious and I didn't hesitate to dive in. A few minutes later I realized how eerily quiet things were.

Looking up, I questioned them. "What, what's wrong?"

Sighing, Jillian replied, "We need to talk, sweetie."

Putting my fork down, I mumbled, "This doesn't

sound good."

"Something happened that night on the farm."

I just stared at them. "A lot fucking happened that night on the farm. You'll have to be more specific."

"Mina, you died. I had to bring you back."

"Wait. What do you mean I died?"

Jillian and Rollo began to explain what had happened. I had scars on my neck from Dixie, but I had no idea it was that bad. The doctors hadn't alluded that they had to bring me back and I told all three of them that.

"You're not listening. I brought you back dear, but with that kind of magic there can be consequences." I nodded for her to continue. "Have you felt the power at all; shifter or wizard?"

I hadn't even thought about it. I was just so relieved to be alive and home. "I, well, I haven't really thought about it at all." My eyes danced in my head as I tried thinking about it.

"You're always cold, Mina. You never used to be cold, at least as long as I've known you."

He was right. "So, I can't shift anymore? I don't

understand."

"Your life force was gone. If someone brings you back, but enough time has passed, those powers can't be reclaimed. Now, sometimes it takes a while, but there's a good chance you've lost your powers."

I covered my face with my hands and began crying. My reaction surprised me. Never in my wildest dreams did I think something like this could happen. I knew there was a possibility one of my powers could overrun the other, but to lose them both entirely had never crossed my mind. Of course, I never expected to have my throat nearly ripped out either.

Jillian rubbed my back and Rollo squeezed my knee. Standing up, I asked for a few moments alone and went up to my room. I stood in front of the mirror and stared at myself. Focusing as hard as I could, I tried to force myself to shift. When that didn't work, I tried to concentrate on the weather outside. Nothing.

Dropping to the bed, I lay there completely numb. Who was I without my shifter side? It was all I'd known and caused me great joy and great strife my entire life. The wizard side was so new to me, but once I was able to control it, it'd saved so many lives—and taken some, too. My brain was on overdrive and I ended up falling asleep from sheer mental exhaustion.

When I woke I found Rollo asleep next to me. His beautiful hair no longer fanned out behind him. I was getting used to his ponytail being gone, but I think part of me would always miss it. I went to touch him and then my brain started messing with me. Would he still want me if I was just a human?

"Stop overthinking, Mina."

My eyes met his and he pulled me close. "Will you still want me if I'm not a shifter?"

"Sweet Mina. When I looked at you I never thought 'Yes, a fellow shifter'. Would you like to know what I thought?" I just nodded. "I thought MINE. I don't care if you're wizard, shifter, human, or serial killer. You're mine."

I started laughing. "Serial killer, really?"

"Well as long as I'm not your killing type."

Giggling, it then dawned on me how rude I'd been to Jillian and Amy the night before. "Jillian and Amy?"

"No worries. When I found you asleep, we cleaned

up and they went home. They're not upset. We all just want what's best for you."

"I can't help but feel guilty about Diane. Why did Jillian's magic work on me and not her?"

He shook his head, "I wish I knew for sure, but Jillian got to you a lot quicker than she did Diane. Things erupted in mass chaos once Diane was shot." He was quiet for a moment before asking, "Have you heard from Debi?"

"No. I need to go see her, but I'm worried she'll hate me."

"She doesn't hate you, Mina. You're probably the one person who can bring her comfort. She was in that hospital room by your side probably as much as I was. She postponed the funeral until you woke up. You should go see her. I can take you."

I knew he was right. Later that day we did just that. After I showered and dressed, Rollo drove me to her apartment, the one she'd shared with Diane. He parked and I walked away. I knocked on her door a few times, but she didn't answer. Remembering I had my own key, I pulled out my keyring and found the one for her door.

Opening the door, I called for her. "Debi? It's Mina. Are you home?"

Her car was parked in the lot downstairs, but that didn't mean anything. I stepped down the hallway as the door to the bathroom opened. Debi stepped out wearing her pajamas and looking worse for wear. When she saw me she burst into tears.

Crying with her, I wrapped my arms around her. "I'm so sorry, Debi. I wish I could bring her back."

We ended up back in her room and sat on the side of her bed. Placing her head on my shoulder she reassured me that she didn't blame me or Jillian.

"Diane was always up for a fight. She went in there knowing full well the risk. You were like a sister to her, too. I'm more upset about having to cover all the rent now."

I gawked at her and we both started laughing. Leave it to Debi to find the humor in any situation. "I'd say you could move in with me, but, yeah." She smiled at me and I knew it was her way of asking for more details. "I don't know. I'm pretty sure my powers are gone. What if he doesn't want me anymore?"

"Oh, my God, Mina. Shut up. If I wasn't straight, I'd want you. That man is head over heels for you. He turned his back on his entire back because of a letter and a hunch that you were worth fighting for. Don't let go of that or I'll claim him for myself."

That was at least the second time she'd teased me about staking claim to him. "Yeah, I get it. It's just going to take some getting used to."

"I know."

"Do you want me to stay or do you want to have a girl's night like we used to?"

"I'd love to, but I'm supposed to work tonight." I looked at my watch and she said, "Yeah, I'm late."

"Well, get to it. You stink. When's the last time you took a shower?"

Shoving me off the bed, she stuck her tongue out at me as I left the room. "Get out of here bitch."

"Will do. We'll stop at Vider's and tell them you're on your way."

"Thank you!"

I closed and locked the door before heading back

down to the truck where Rollo was waiting for me. Climbing in, I closed the distance between us and kissed him with everything I had. He was momentarily surprised, but immediately began kissing me back. We hadn't been together since all hell broke loose and I needed him.

"Mina, let's go home."

Sighing, "I want that, but we have to swing by Vider's first. I promised Debi."

Groaning, he threw the truck into drive and headed toward Vider's. Once Debi arrived and we were sure she was fine we got the hell out of there.

ROLLO

That night it was different with her. We were both different. Something had changed between us and it was even better than it had been before. I pulled her on top of me and guided my way inside her. Her eyes closed as we both groaned.

Only Love by Mumford & Sons played through the speakers and it was almost a short retelling of our romance. I'd fallen so quickly for her, only to let her down. The fact that she'd forgiven me was my only saving grace. Slowly, her hips rocked back and forth against mine.

Running her hands up my arms, her hands found mine as we intertwined our fingers. Her mouth found mine as our tongues and bodies moved to the same rhythm. Her back arched as she got lost in the sensations. My lips captured her nipple as she squeezed her fingers tight around my own.

Her moans and gasps nearly undid me. I wanted her again and I hadn't even finished with round one. She changed the motion of her hips and I knew what she was doing. She liked to draw it out, enjoying the restraint it took to avoid coming. She truly was a vixen.

"Mina. We have all night and the rest of our lives. Come for me."

She sat up and I took advantage of it, circling my thumb over her clit as she moaned. "Rollo..."

Her legs began to tremble against my hips and I knew she was ready to break apart. Thrusting up into her harder over and over again until I felt her entire body begin to quiver. No longer able to hold herself up, my arms encased her as I continued fucking her.

"Rollo, don't stop."

She cried out as I whispered in her ear. "I love feeling you soak me as you come. I love you, Mina." Her cries and whimpers were telling as her walls clamped down on me. "I'm gonna cum, Mina."

She lifted her face in search of my mouth. As her tongue caressed mine, I groaned out my release. She swiveled her hips ever so gently and milked every drop from me. I was spent, yet still hard.

Looking at me curiously, she inquired, "Didn't you...?"

Smiling, I flipped her to her back and sank back into her. "Yes, I did. I just need you again."

In the Spring, we finally got word that they were going to exhume Scott's body in the next few days. Mina stared at me, almost as if she had forgotten about it. We had come to terms with the fact that we may never have the answers we needed or wanted and we were ok with that.

"Rollo, I think we should let him—Scott or Jude, whoever it is—rest in peace."

I searched her eyes and knew she was right. "Ok. I'll take care of it."

After a lot of thought and consideration we'd moved into the farmhouse and had sold Mina's house. With Zeke and Victoria dead, I got an inheritance I wasn't expecting and we used the money to fix up Scott's house. The money had been my father's so I didn't feel like it was bad karma on my part to accept it.

I'd had a successful winter with the plow service and had begun picking up some new clients. Now we were busy preparing for a summer of landscape work. My life had become so peaceful not having a pack to worry about.

We never saw or heard from Dixie again and we weren't worried about it. Some of the pack had come crawling back and a few I welcomed, but let them know I wasn't a leader. A few were ok with it and others left. Some were just too accustomed to pack life and couldn't function without it.

Some of the guys stayed and moved together into a house nearby together. A couple came to work for me and another went to work at the local mechanic's shop. The same guy also caught Debi's eye.

I stood in the driveway and stared at the spot where I thought I'd lost Mina forever. The sound of her voice broke me from my memories as I walked to the house. She met me at the door and flung her arms around me.

"You're in a good mood. What's going on?"

"So, you're sure you don't want to be pack leader?"

Where was this coming from? "I told you, my pack leading days are behind me." Pursing her lips I was starting to become suspicious. "Did one of the guys come and talk to you? I'll kill 'em."

Giggling, she denied it. "No. It's nothing." Walking away from me, I knew it wasn't nothing.

I clasped my hands around her waist and pulled her back against me. "What is it, Mina? You can tell me."

She took my hand in hers and placed it low on her

belly. "It's just that soon we're going to have a pack of our own." She remained still and waited for my reaction.

Her powers had never come back, shifter or magic, and she'd come to accept it. Me, I couldn't care less. She'd also remembered Jude touching her the night he died and her being slammed back against the wall. That had been the moment he returned her magic to her. Now her words had me scrambling for their meaning. Turning her in my arms I searched her eyes.

"Wait, you're...?"

Pressing her lips together in a straight line, she raised her brows and nodded. "I'm pregnant." I was speechless. "Rollo, say something. Are you mad?"

"Mad?"

"I just, I know we said we would wait, but apparently pulling out isn't one hundred percent effective."

We both laughed knowing we'd agreed to wait, but had also not taken proper precautions. "I'm not mad. Maybe a little shocked, but not mad." Grabbing her arm, I pulled her close. "How far along?"

"Only six or eight weeks. It's early. I have an appointment next week."

Cupping her face, I tilted her mouth up to mine and kissed her. "You're feeling ok?"

Nodding, she confirmed, "Yes."

That night I watched her sleep, my hand resting on her belly. So many people had tried taking us down and while we never got all the answers, Mina got her revenge, I got my revenge. There was nothing sweeter than knowing we'd come out the victors and the guilty had paid. Thank God for that letter. I didn't want to think about where I'd be without it.

Now a child. I wondered if the gene would lie dormant or not. Jillian had told us a few months back that Mina still carried both genes so odds were high that any child of hers, ours, would inherit it. Then Mina had asked what I hadn't thought of.

"If Jude was able to keep my power inside him, could I do the same if my child had the Thomas magic?"

Jillian thought about it for a moment and then said, "Yes, I would have to say probably so."

"How soon would I know?"

Jillian smiled, "Usually during pregnancy. Maybe as soon as the first trimester. It's different for every wizard. I felt it sooner with Jude than I did his sisters. You just never know."

At that moment Mina took in a deep breath and when I looked to her face, her eyes were that bright white blue for a split second before they went back to their beautiful blue.

"Mina? Are you ok?"

She smiled and put my hand back on her belly and covered it with her own. "He has magic!"

"He?"

"Yes, he told me. And he's shifter, too."

Tears filled my eyes. A son. She was giving me a son who'd have the magic powers from both of us. Life couldn't get any better.

PLAYLIST

Alive by Sia

Maneater by Grace Mitchell

Monster by Lady Gaga

End Of All Days by Thirty Seconds To Mars

Nightcall by Kavinsky

Rescue My Heart by Liz Longley

Infinity by The xx

Poison by Vaults

Hurricane by Thirty Seconds To Mars

Seven Devils by Florence + The Machine

Only Love by Mumford & Sons

Thank you so much for taking the time to read my novella from **Woodland Creek**!

All reviews are appreciated.

If you would like to read more from the *Woodland Creek* series, please click on the link below:

http://woodlandcreekseries.com

More from J.M. Witt

The Anchored Hearts Series

Letting Go (Vol. 1)

Hiding Away (Vol. 1.5)

Letting Go of You (Vol. 2)

Fading Away (Vol. 2.5)

Letting Go of Us (Vol. 3)

The Blind Vows Series

Trust, Honor, Love: (Vol. 1)

Body, Heart, Soul: (Vol. 2)

About the Author

J.M. resides in Metro Detroit, MI with her husband and four young children.

Always wanting to write romance novels, she followed her dreams after having baby #4, who may or may not be the spawn of Christian Grey!

She hopes you'll enjoy more than a good book, but have an experience.

You can find her at

www.jmwittbooks.com

Twitter @wittymomauthor

www.facebook.com/jmwittbooks

www.ingramcontent.com/pod-product-compliance
Lightning Source LLC
Chambersburg PA
CBHW020615180626
46810CB00007B/2787

* 9 7 8 0 6 9 2 5 6 1 5 1 5 *